MW01093486

"*Hot Girls with Balls* is a thrillingly cheeky, tenderly irreverent, seriously funny novel, anchored by a loving duo I couldn't stop rooting for and featuring a very spicy send-up of the comments section. No one is spared from Benedict Nguyễn's dishy satire, but with writing this alive, we wouldn't want it any other way."

CHANTAL V. JOHNSON, author of *Post-Traumatic*

"Benedict Nguyễn's *Hot Girls with Balls* is so fun, so adrenalized, as grippy as Pilates socks, that it seems a little unfair that it's also smart as hell. It's a novel that's utterly contemporary, vividly specific, funny, and moving. Nguyễn has given us a kinetic, deeply pleasurable satire that I'll be pressing into many hands, this volleyball season and after."

SARAH THANKAM MATHEWS, author of *All This Could Be Different*

"Nguyễn serves up sharp, hilarious satire about trans celebrity and the limits and costs of trying to change a world from within it. I've never read such an unflinching celebration of the weird, violent poetry of online trans discourse, and was here for Six and Green's journey—via fierce tournament play, lesbian processing, brand deals and soaring follower counts—somehow to rise above it."

JEANNE THORNTON, author of *Summer Fun* and *A/S/L*

Hot Girls with Balls

Hot Girls

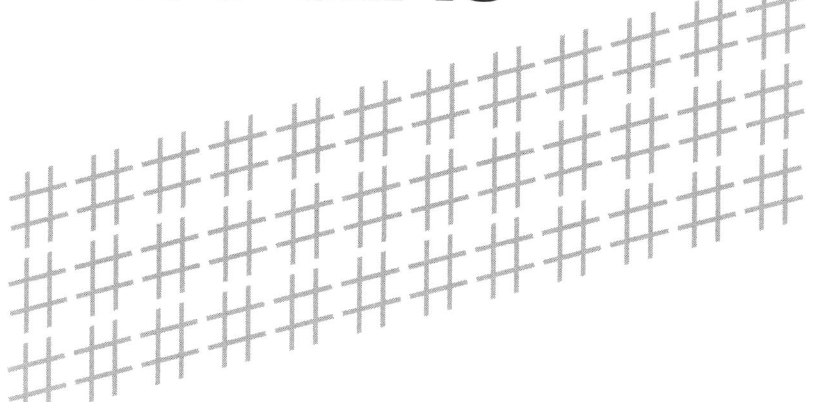

with Balls

A Novel

Benedict Nguyễn

Catapult
New York

HOT GIRLS WITH BALLS

This is a work of fiction. All of the characters, organizations, and events portrayed in this novel are either products of the author's imagination or are used fictitiously.

First Catapult edition: 2025

Grateful acknowledgment for reprinting materials is made to the following: David Sansone, excerpt from *Greek Athletics and the Genesis of Sport.* Copyright © 1988 by The Regents of the University of California. Reprinted with the permission of University of California Press Books. Anelise Chen, *So Many Olympic Exertions.* Copyright © 2017 by Anelise Chen. Reprinted with the permission of Kaya Press.

ISBN: 978-1-64622-247-6

Library of Congress Control Number: 2024951087

Jacket design by Sarah Brody
Jacket images: net © Shutterstock / W001X;
balls © Shutterstock / maximmmmum
Book design by tracy danes

Catapult
New York, NY
books.catapult.co

Printed in the United States of America

10 9 8 7 6 5 4 3 2 1

For Julia, Susan, and Georgiana

Even today we are still likely, it is true, to refer gleefully to the baiting of a particularly gullible colleague as "great sport."

DAVID SANSONE,
Greek Athletics and the Genesis of Sport

I was always prepared for someone to call out to me and try to get me to join some team. It was both a recurring fantasy and a recurring nightmare.

ANELISE CHEN,
So Many Olympic Exertions

Contents

AUTHOR'S NOTE

Deep breaths, dear reader: the language in this novel is a bit violent at times, and if you need a little time-out, that's *totally* okay :)

DIG

NO ONE COULD THINK STRAIGHT BECAUSE EVERYONE was actually gay. At least, that was how the kids on Flitter complained about a year of the COVIS pandemic frying their brains. And they weren't wrong. For example, one Sunday the following text scrolled below two very hot gay girls' faces across so many beaming screens:

omgggggg this is so adorable, my heart is literally MELTING!

Obsessed! With! You! Two!!

Why are you wearing a shirt? Show us the titties!

Pinned: @everyourgreen @sixsosweet ~Six & Green~ 4/19/21

@6nGreenENVIES and 34,987 others joined

Omg! Yes Green, the strength! I can see your pelvic floor!

I can't wait to see their rematch IN-PERSON at the Sonus tournament in 3 weeks!

I like Six more because I love a manly tall girl and would you look at her shoulders?!

Last year's lockdown match made me bawl and I'm still not over it!

@everyourgreen! What do you put in your smoothies? Also, next time, can you film without socks?

Can we talk about Six's jaw today? What artist sculpted that face? Who do I vinmo a tip?

Fucking chink faggot dyke dipshits! Go back to your country! Or the closet!

I like Green more because I like a lithe little lady who can give you some force when you fuck her.

Omg, I didn't know Six's voice was so high pitched, it's so cute!

Omg a cis white racist! Everyone block @badboybryan

Omg why do you have to pit women against each other? Just love them both

Our baby girl @sixsosweet was sick and Green was across the globe?

Yeah! And Green's shorter but has that sexy girl baritone, it's so hot

Wait, so they're dudes who "identify as women" but play for the boys' league? Woke-ism is running out of ideas

@badboybryan if you hate them so much, then why are you watching their show?? Just log off you little bigot shit!

Yeah, @badboybryan you should follow @transaretrans to learn more

These babes play on rival teams too!?
6&G 5eva! 6&G 5eva! 6&G 5eva!

And this was just what people wrote on the main feed.

Now, indoor volleyball's favorite sweethearts were no longer on Instagraph Live, but they were still online. Six (@sixsosweet, 27, the taller soft butch, Lublin, Poland) was exasperated but was deciding how to convey it on SpaceTime, where her girlfriend Green (@everyourgreen, 28, the shorter but still tall high femme, Santa Cruz, USA) was still peeling off her Live Grin. It always took Green longer than Six to relax that precise smile she put on to broadcast for her fans. Six's face muscles were taut but always relaxed, even as she pouted about the petty fight she didn't want to start. She wanted to have a mature discussion.

They hadn't cultivated a long-distance friendship for seven years and long-distance romance for nearly two years without learning how to communicate their feelings. Six began, I know we have the calendar. I know it's just a little show that we do every week. But if we're actually having a disagreement, even if it's a small one, why can't we just bring that into the Live? Why can't our show evolve with us?

I mean, we agreed on a narrative arc, Green said. If we introduce little blips into it now, we'll have to answer to them later. Do you really want to talk about how I didn't check in when you got sick a few days ago a week from now?

Six watched as forehead tension replaced Green's Live Grin. Before their show, Six (the more sensitive one) had asked if they could talk about it and Green (the more calculating one) had taken the request as a request and not an assertion, and so, responded with a definitive No. They would stick to the score. After all, Six's sore throat had passed. The COVIS test had come back negative. Green's minor negligence didn't have discrete consequences on Six's physical health. But then, they couldn't evaluate their relationship health with a nasal swab.

Tonight, some thirty-eight thousand devices across six continents had tuned in to the weekly Instagraph Live show *Six & Green* to watch its two stars, the happiest of long-distance couples, talk about their skin care routines (sponsored), getting body work done between travel (not sponsored), and the latest TV period romances (one unofficially sponsored). The live viewer count had dipped slightly from last week but their managers cared more about the twenty-four-hour play count anyway.

What's more, Green (the more anxious one) continued, I don't want to air out the actual concerns of our relationship live for strangers to gossip about. If they're gonna speculate, they should fantasize about the fantasy we create for them, not what we're actually going through.

What? Six (the less online one) asked. I don't get it. She looked past the camera as the image of her face danced in and out of the late evening light. She momentarily forgot where this week's away game had taken her.

This fight about whether they could publicly fight in front of their audience should've been too meta. But really, it was astounding it had taken the two of them this long to have this talk. While Green posted more, she also valued her privacy.

To Six, online or offline, life was life and filtering was a ruse. While they both saw their live show as just another performance, hundreds of thousands of viewers so wanted it to be real. They wanted it so badly to be real.

Green's face had frozen in the sun-soaked glow of her hotel room in Salt Lake City. She would've recoiled at the sight of her half-open mouth but Six found the unintended image endearing as she remembered she was in Leipzig this week.

Are you there? Six asked as she tried to remember where she had walked that afternoon.

Green's face began glimmering in motion again. Yeah. What I mean is, I'm not sorry about wanting to keep our private life private, she said, her voice persistently flat. They had worked on apologizing less to each other but defensiveness wasn't cute either.

I didn't ask you to apologize, Six said, her chipper cadence allowing just a chirp of irritation to register. Not that their improv coach Guthrie ever had to work on Six's vocal facility; it was Green who had to learn how to sound like That Bitch only when she wanted to. Though they never practiced serious arguments like this one. Just cutesy, algorithm-friendly brattiness.

Green seemed to realize she'd miscalibrated. Seeing Six walking outside, she asked, Are you sure you're feeling better?

I'm off tomorrow but I won't stay out late. Six looked away from her camera again as she crossed an unfamiliar street.

Babe, that's not what I asked, Green said.

Oh, I know. Sorry. Six grinned.

Green knew the apology was also a pardon. Maybe Six

wasn't so upset. They would be fine. Just two more weeks and a tournament before lovers' summer.

Looking down at her phone, Six saw Green's smile between her hands, felt the love and concern through the three million pixels recreating this facsimile of her girlfriend. Holding her phone like this made it both easier and harder to forget that their future depended on people using their own tiny devices to pay for an exclusive but open-access view into the mirage.

Yeah, the whole team is off tomorrow, Six went on. But my PT cleared me to go back to practice on Tuesday. And my throat will be smoother than your best set.

Aww. Is your ankle still sore? Green asked.

Barely. I'll probably still take it easy tomorrow, which won't help my campaign to start in time for Sonus, but having a few days off definitely helped. Six had landed a contract with the most renowned team in the league, Czwartek, only to spend the entire season on the backup bench.

Are you still shooting with Clara this week?

Six nodded. She's flying a whole crew out!

Green's Live Grin was back. Green had the ballerina legs. Not Six with her great big calves. Glancing at her own elegant gastrocnemii, Green replied, That's great, sweetie!

As Six made sure not to trip through the barely lit park she'd passed by earlier, an organic lull entered the chat, allowing Green to remind herself that Six's collab with Clara or walking for Dulce & Gabbano's fashion week last month wasn't just because of her higher follower count. Rather it was probably also her image (more trendily genderfluid than Green) and/or her height (six inches taller). Maybe it was also Six's rounder eyes and signature wing that simply did not work with Green's eyes. The world loved delicate eyeliner on someone like Six, with her commanding figure and shapely shoulders. Who wanted a slightly fishier trans girl with predictably slender shoulders like Green (722k followers) when you could have a seductively androgynous trans woman like Six (876k followers) on your runway? Green wasn't self-deprecating, just honest about what she looked like.

If she had proof Six's extra followers made the difference, Green would have to start an inane conversation pointing out how the imbalance had more significant, ever quantifiable implications on their livelihoods. And if Six and Green couldn't patch this little not-argument, who would field more sponsorship requests after their breakup? Certainly not the one with fewer followers. Perhaps their relative difference in fame didn't even register with Six because the imbalance favored her. Why notice what doesn't affect you? Six barely had to try and Green tried so, so hard.

Green's minor musing was interrupted by the sound of Six's shoes hitting pavement again. Green could hear the clop of one of the custom pairs (size 47 EU) Dulce had gifted her. Maybe Six looked weary or maybe the inconsistent lighting blurred her face enough for Green to project her own fears onto her girlfriend.

Before Green could decide whether to return to their not-fight, Six rescued her. I'm sorry, she said. I didn't mean to make this that deep. You know I'm a drama queen when I get sick and there wasn't much that you could've done really. Just hearing from you would've been nice, but we just needed to talk about this between us.

Green's gratitude overpowered her guilt. While Six had escalated the tussle to this point, she had also deflated it so gracefully.

I'm sorry I didn't let you know I was overwhelmed, Green said. Since we had canceled our SpaceTimes, I just . . . I know I know better.

It's okay, Greenie. And you're right. Nobody wants to see us do lesbian processing every week. If we're gonna do this show, it needs to stand alone, not like a real-real reality show.

Since premiering nine months ago, *Six & Green* offered viewers an escape from the gruesome mortality so palpable in all the other half hours of the day. Who wouldn't root for Six and Green? They were trans women and stars of the men's global volleyball league. They were in a long-distance relationship. They were proudly Asian American (no hyphen) in an era of resurgent hate as a global pandemic persisted, killing so many in its wake. Its observably sleek production indicated that they didn't deny how they were largely protected from the worst of its consequences. Even so, Six and Green counted among their fans the most romantic and the most cynical. Everyone needed a realist narrative of seemingly insurmountable hurdles overcome to give them hope. Could Green help Six install shelves in her living room over Instagraph Live? By the seventeen-minute mark, the drill had pierced the wall. Whether earnest or ironic, whether appointment phone-TV or shameful pleasure, views were views.

Green nodded, the corners of her Live Grin relaxing once

again as she swallowed the conversation she didn't know how to continue right now. Had she had Six's full attention, Six probably would've seen her girlfriend slipping on and off that eerie persona while she was supposed to be off the clock. But Six was just blissfully breathing in tree-filtered oxygen. Half-heartedly, Green said, If you want to talk about it more, we totally can. Maybe we need to tap into the trans dyke audience who want to watch us process?

Six looked to see Green's worry. The offer was probably empty and the joke was definitely glib, and still, Six missed her girlfriend. Aww, thanks, babe.

Green could see Six was just being nice. Six took in the image of Green facing the window, the length of her jaw in high relief. Her hair's relentless straightness made her signature high ponytail easy to put up, easy to make shine. Her rounded nose was so cute and so elegant, she wanted to lean her lips through and nibble. Her face looked like that and she had to file as a Boy for her Job. Even Six and Green found it funny sometimes.

Never mind physical prowess; Six and Green were ideal ambassadors for the sport of indoor men's volleyball because they were both beautiful. Six's wavy hair was too big and unruly to pull off Green's pony but the three French braids that combined at the base of her neck became her signature. Where Six's round face was all soft curves and spacious cheeks prime for makeup, Green's was divinely proportioned angles. This was pro sports but it was also entertainment, and hot people sold more tickets than average-looking people.

Now, they just smiled at each other, blearily but with affection. Refreshed by her evening stroll and the sight of her darling's less tense face, Six decided to let their tiny argument go. Her team had won without needing her and maybe she'd taken that out on Green.

Six and Green could've passed minutes like this, just staring at each other, not needing to say aloud the obvious thing: they missed each other. They loved each other. But still, people said pointless, obvious things to each other all the time.

Like: You have practice? Six said.

Yeah, the bus leaves in an hour. Green tried to sigh quietly, not wanting to complain to Six, who had a real reason to resent practice this season. Though Six had negotiated a raise from her previous six-figure contract, she still made less than Green, a starting setter for Regalado, one of Czwartek's main rivals in the league.

Play hard for me, beanie, Six said, wistfully. She called Green *beanie* because even though Green was shorter, she had tall person energy, like a bean pole.

Of course, Green smiled, meekly. Gotta get ready to beat you again at Sonus. Wait, Sixy, are you dressed for the rain?

Six nodded and angled her phone to show her oversized pearlescent kelly green puffer. You're sweet to worry, but I'm not letting this cough linger any longer. Go have a good practice, darling! And good game! Good morningnight!

Good nightmorning, little lady! Green echoed. She called Six little lady because, well, sometimes obvious irony was effective. When the call ended, Six imagined the image of her girlfriend bouncing out the door as it might appear on her phone screen. Six thought about how much twice-daily video chats sustained their relationship and their careers. They nudged each other through the monotony of chronic soreness and jet lag around the globe. They planned their show and, as of late, their future. Every jetsetter needs a routine to tether them. Six and Green stretched the singularity of space time to beam into each other's mornings and evenings, their circadian clocks in a forever canon.

###

A couple days later, Six was back in Lublin and Green prepared to fly to Denver for her weekend game. Green's agent Yemma forwarded her a rough cut of the video edit from yesterday's practice, noting the time stamps of her screen time. Seated at her desk, Green scooched her ass back and leaned her head into the screen, the better to admire a close-up of her face on her 13-inch laptop, which could only display the 4K footage in 1080p, but still, she needed to see if she looked good. For the confessional, the crew had scooted a cart of balls to appear just behind the net framing her left side. She paused the video and zoomed in on her forehead, where, next to a droplet of sweat, she could make out the faintest scar from a breakout she'd had two weeks ago. She was certainly vain, but this tiny spot wasn't the problem. Her team (as in, not volleyball) would edit this out for her personal Instagraph. The problem was how washed-out she looked. Of Japanese heritage, she was paler with blue undertones compared to Six's Vietnamese tan with reddish undertones. Even so, Green wasn't this pale. Green could not have Regalado's marketing compromise Green's marketing. Her contract was up next year. She might relocate, might get aged out by some twenty-two-year-old child. She thought of Alan on Six's team. Poor Six. Green loved her job but had to prepare for the time when her time on the court would end. Green as a brand would have to be ready. The rich had bills too! Her starting salary was higher than Six's but who knew how much Six made from her brand deals? Green would need more of her own partnerships and brand deals to find out. They were the kind of nouveau riche couple who talked in terms of vague financial goals instead of numbers.

Green wrote to her agent:

> Hi Yemma, I look washed-out, don't I?
> Can we color correct me so I don't look ill?
> Thanks love you!
> Green

###

At the Czwartek home arena across the world, it was morning. A bent-over Six (#6, 6'7", 204 lbs., middle blocker) swung her arms behind her ass and bounded into the air, her arms propelling her armpits clear above the net, her thick braid twirling behind her. Across the net, Alan (#4, 6'6", 198 lbs., outside hitter) slapped the ball and it bent Six's fingertips back. Its trajectory was too fast, too high for any of her fellow second stringers in the back row to catch it.

Yes! Exactly! That's it, Alan! Coach Pete said.

What Pete didn't say, whether out of ignorance or condescension, was that Six had had plenty of time to telegraph Alan's move, even if she hadn't known his play, a block out. Alan wasn't slow. If anything, Six felt slow, and was probably slowing. Rather it was that Alan still moved with amateurish predictability; the alignment of his line of sight and plane of his right wrist swing betrayed his plan before Six had to even think about bending her knees. Sure, he might fake out, but he had yet to set that precedent. Six could've stopped the ball blindfolded if she wanted. But right now, her job was to hold back and help their Baby-Faced Opposite Hitter practice this most basic move. Obviously, Czwartek was thinking long game with him.

While Alan was already starting at twenty-two years old, he wasn't the one in her way. It was Sam, the second middle blocker who was yawning just behind him. Watching him stretch his pathologically sedentary lower back, Six held in her own yawn.

All right, one more time, Pete called. This time, Six, you can try to block him a bit more. What Pete meant was, Look like you're trying just a bit harder, but still let him get the point so we can build Baby's confidence up.

Alan smiled sheepishly, almost apologetically, at Six through the net. Six obviously wasn't a gender essentialist but this was a boy among men! Real men! If Six were being held back by this floppy-haired, goofy-cheeked newbie, she'd have quit. He'd be easier to hate if he were a talentless nepo baby like Green's teammate Griffin. Most of Alan's instincts were pretty good. He'd stumbled into volleyball when he was fourteen and his high school coach helped him fundraise for a summer clinic, where he caught the attention of some college coaches. It was actually Six's former San José coaches who'd given him the full scholarship that rescued him from a downtrodden town where he otherwise would've lived his whole life. Before volleyball, he'd sincerely wanted to become a plumber. While it was an important job, you couldn't become a millionaire before thirty by installing faucets.

It wasn't Alan's fault that Six's excellence was continually taken for granted. He was just there. Nor could she really blame Sam and James. They'd been Czwartek's starting middles for years. Seniority was timeless. Barring COVIS or injury from Sam or James, Six would "stay warm" on the warm-up bike for the Sonus Tournament. As Six prepared for another approach, James nodded at her sympathetically. But was the expression on Sam's face a smirk?

A younger, less talented player might rejoice at getting subbed in at around the 19-point mark, if a team was sufficiently ahead in pool play. Such a dude could help the team to 25 points, only to get swapped out when the next set began. If Czwartek won the first three sets out in a row, which they did reasonably often against lower-ranked teams, this might amount to five minutes of play time per set, or fifteen minutes a match. Over six matches in pool play, it could add up to a paltry ninety minutes of game time in a whole tournament. At most! But when Six was on La Spezia, she'd played every match all match. Six would not settle for sympathy court time.

After a few more goes of Alan thwacking the ball at different angles toward Six's fingers and forearms, Six let herself show the slightest hint of weariness. She hoped the coaching staff wasn't focused on her massaging her knees. This wasn't an inordinate amount of jumping but she wasn't Alan's age anymore.

At least Six's salary reflected her contribution to Alan's development. It had made renting a brand-new, two-floor apartment in Lublin's most thoroughly gentrified district seem like the most prudent choice. Six never cooked, never did her own laundry, and could take a car anywhere, including her team's home arena just blocks away. Though if she wasn't getting game time, she was at least going to walk everywhere.

She couldn't tell if she'd even have the endurance to start again. Did she need more reps or more rest? She'd survived COVIS but had no idea how much residual viral deterioration was wreaking havoc in her circulatory system. At 27, she neared the age in a professional volleyball player's career where her physical peak was either approaching or just past. What kept players on teams, besides sturdy joints, was the wisdom and maturity to play smarter than their younger and faster teammates. On a new team, seniority had Six aging ahead but falling behind. Before the assistant coach's whistle finished its toot, Six was up, bouncing between her two feet, pretending her legs were thick springs ready to bounce back.

###

If intimate relationships were a sport, Six and Green's twice-daily calls were the twenty squeezes on the grip strength toy Six's physical therapist had sent her or the knee alignment exercises assigned by Green's trainer. Even if this kind of maintenance felt a little rote, it was nonetheless intentional and effective.

On this SpaceTime, Six was complaining about two-hour flights. But, my cough's gone, she beamed. How was practice yesterday, babe?

Because Green had such an early morning, they had skipped their call last nightmorning.

Oh, the usual. Green rolled her eyes. Griffin still hurls himself after the ball when it's already a lost cause and Oliver just nods and says, Good fight. Like, how can they see his practice stats and still let him start?

Six nodded sympathetically. I feel like he barely touches the ball when y'all play, she said, as if this was a point neither had ever made to each other before.

Truly useless. We might as well just be a six-person team.

It didn't help that Green was so good at receiving and thus often made up for Griffin's ineptitude. Shorter than Six (by six inches), Green could get lower than most attackers to dig, could zip across the backcourt in so many efficient strides. When she was in the front row and Griffin failed to convert, the coaches just tossed off the lost point.

Green went on, We didn't get our jobs because our dads' companies sponsored our teams. I wish he would transfer so Will could play.

Will was the second-string libero. At 6'1", he was the same height as Green (two inches taller than Griffin) but even nimbler, his spritely legs propelling his body to the right spot every time. When they scrimmaged, the difference between his and Griffin's abilities was painful to watch. If Will's family weren't based in Santa Cruz, maybe he would've left by now. Instead, Six got to empathize with him running laps during the time-outs.

If Griffin's spot could be bought, the promise of Six-driven ticket sales should've been enough to put her on the court. It wasn't just embarrassing. Relegating Six to spectating her own games was bad business. To her girlfriend she said, Or Czwartek could poach him!

You wouldn't! Green feigned a scandalous look.

I don't know, I heard Pete might be scouting.

Little lady, worry about your own game!

Six gasped in comic rage. I'm working on it, babe!

It wasn't special banter but it was familiar and kept them in shape. When Green talked about her team's filmed practice, she didn't bring up the rough cut she'd already received. Now that Six was a sometimes model, Green felt silly waving her provincial vanities in her girlfriend's face. Six didn't ask whether Green had been a focal point for the camera, because, well, obviously. The conversation was mindless enough for Six to remember Sunday's almost-fight. Traveling back to Lublin made it feel like weeks ago. But tonight, they were both too tired and so Six left the sore spot alone and asked her girlfriend, How'd you play?

Green talked about how great she felt, how glamorous the shots were. Peace was maintained through inertia. Between their day jobs that kept them on tour and their budding empire that kept them planning their upcoming content, lover time had been subsumed by girlboss time. Instead of soothing each other's late-night anxieties, they shared their little recaps and Six helped Green with the exercises their improv coach Guthrie set them.

Tonight, Green waited groggily at the airport and Six was endless miles away lying in bed at the hotel and the next time, maybe Green would be at the hotel and Six at the arena, the definite article foregrounding the monotony of soulless rooms and beds that all felt the same. So many people envied their jetsetting jobs but really Six didn't even do much sightseeing. When discussing this on a Live, she had deadpanned: I need to keep wandering the globe because my parents were refugees and I have intergenerational trauma.

Wait, how's your cough, little lady? Green asked. Did you just have practice?

Oh, it's better! Thanks, beanie. Did I not say? And yeah, I just practiced this morning.

I don't think so? Green said. Unless I spaced?

Yeah, no, my throat feels amazing. Like, I don't even notice it.

Aww babe, I'm so glad!

Sensing Six's eyes fluttering shut, Green wished Six a good nightmorning. Six said good morningnight. Green dragged her carry-on down the ramp and Six dragged her arm across the bed to turn the light off.

###

Before her plane took off, Green watched an updated edit of the video, skipping to the cue point of her cool-toned but now rosier face on her screen. She nodded at the moving image of herself smiling and sweating through breezy statements about preparing her body to peak for Sonus. She felt a little sore from playing more but it felt good to be sore, blah blah blah. Guthrie had helped her voice sound more gratefully surprised and less smug. Now that her skin looked the way she wanted it to look—neither aspirationally white nor falsely exotic—she focused on the stiffness above her jaw as she spoke. She still couldn't manage to let it relax on camera. She texted Guthrie asking to meet separately to work on it before their next Live.

Across the world, as sleepy as Six was, she couldn't actually sleep when she crumpled into the dark. Her brain sometimes got pent-up energy too, and she wasn't ready to discuss this question with her partner yet: What would she and Green have in common if they weren't both Asian American trans women and pro volleyball players? It was an impossible hypothetical. Because they had so many shared experiences, Six couldn't fathom not being tied to Green for the rest of her life. They'd been friends seven years. And Six couldn't imagine dating anyone else. Or rather, she couldn't imagine anyone willing to put up with her travel schedule having good intentions. Who would want to date a hot girl who could both destroy you with her womanhood and beat you at sports? Six didn't want a perpetually intimidated lover. For all of her extra six inches (of height), Six knew she didn't intimidate Green. Even with her frustrations, that truth was still refreshing. But maybe it came at the cost of Green not taking her seriously enough either.

Six admired Green's ambition, even if she didn't always relate to it. She had chosen to transfer teams and move countries to take her game to the next level, not impress other people. Maybe if she'd been starting like she was supposed to, she could've channeled her drive toward Green's vision for them. Maybe if they'd met without volleyball, it would've been Green who felt perplexed by Six wanting more and more and more. In this universe though, Six was sure. If their relationship was going to evolve, better as lovers than enemies.

Earlier, they'd talked through the episode two weeks from now: It'd be the night before the first match of the tournament. Six and Green would express the sheer gratitude for how life-affirming their lives got to be. Win or lose, they had already cemented their intertwined legacy as world-famous Asian Americans, as trans girlies in men's sport, as athletes vital to the resurgence of volleyball in the nation-state that had first founded it.

Before Six and Green, volleyball was at best a tertiary sport in America. Volleyball moved faster than soccer (points were scored) but slower than basketball (a volleyball match could last up to three hours). It lacked football's flashy violence but deployed tennis's technology to dramatize which side of a line a ball fell on. Volleyball required both force and elegance, fast reflexes and deep patience to direct a ball to victory. Like in baseball, players had no reason to bodycheck each other, but the field of play was more condensed. It wasn't just balls but endless unspoken feeling filtering back and forth across the net.

To a few anonymous tech bros and former college players,

volleyball was both an underappreciated sport and an underexploited market. A decade ago they threw parties for their industry friends and played volleyball on big-screen televisions while talking casually about how football, baseball, and even basketball had been corrupted by steroids and betting scandals. They had seen headlines of Six and Green, but when they launched the Sonus Volleyball Network on ESTN the year Six went pro, these bros had no idea how symbiotic the success of their company and these young women's careers would be. That first season, they just wanted to show viewers how to watch their beloved sport anew. They hired a DP to capture slo-mo close-ups of sinewy bodies glistening with heterosexual exertion. They hired commentators to talk about players like TV characters with recurring flaws that might just be redeemed. They knew their audience. Tailgating sports bros would never admit it, but Sunday Night Football was both their reality TV and prestige drama.

And it worked. Each year's profits improved on the last. In 2020, the tech bros' strategic investment culminated in the revival of a global tournament that hadn't taken place since 1984. Inviting the highest-ranked clubs from each regional league, Sonus would crown the best team in the world. They created the Sonus Volleyball Tournament and spared no expense in the twelve-camera coverage, yielding endless hours of content whose gems they edited into packages sent to outlets worldwide.

So while the advent of COVIS eliminated Sonus's ticket revenue, it unlocked a new fanbase. The microcosm of volleyball fans infected the American internet. Diehards made universal the catharsis of Six leaping from behind the three-meter line to spike the ball with the most elastic snap of her arched back. Videos of Six swinging her shoulder around the full range of its socket to produce that life-giving smack didn't just populate virtual surfaces. Through fiber optics and 4K screens, Six took every spectator's repressed sweat and wrung it out through her own pores. When Green set, she wasn't just passing the ball, she was physicalizing the beauty and precision of human agency. All for the fans.

But neither Six nor Green had come into volleyball to bear the burden of humanity's unfulfilled needs. They'd simply been handed balls. Six's parents worked demanding jobs and the neighbor who babysat her, a starting varsity opposite at the local high school, showed her the basics. Green's parents didn't play but her aunties and uncles did. At her first faceball, a supposedly errant spike from a cousin, she skittered back. But so thoroughly shamed as a boy to remain unflinching in all scenarios, she'd just shaken her head twice before learning how to defend her skull.

And relentlessly, their journeys into boy ball persisted. Across time zones, they had two parallel realizations: First, they were actually girls. Six told her babysitter first, who hugged her and told her she was a talented young woman. Green told her cousins, who loudly whispered about it in front of her parents, who then asked Green to confirm. Second, they would still have to play on the boys' team. Biology and bigotry were insurmountable, made-up forces. Luckily, Six and Green were bro-y girls who enjoyed the more aggressive rhythms of men's volleyball.

And so, by the time they made their high school varsity teams (Green as a sophomore, Six as a junior), they were the young women on young men's teams they never thought they could be. They sacrificed their bodies to the kind of puberty their sport demanded of them but in their hearts, they knew who they were. It should seem fantastical, but it was truly just coincidental. People had gender feelings all the time. Because Six and Green proclaimed their feelings assuredly, they made it normal. Before their existence became a tidbit of national collegiate sport news, the conversations they'd had with their angsty boy teammates proceeded with indifference.

Trust me, a newly 6'5" Six said.

I am not attracted to any of you, a stubbornly 6'1" Green said.

Even before meeting, these exceptionally tall Asian women shattered trans glass ceilings in near sync.

For college, Green flew from Dallas to Lancaster for a scholarship on the first-ranked team in the league. Her freshman season, she skipped ahead of a waiting junior to take a just-graduated senior's spot as starting setter. As a senior in high school, Six had seen headlines of Green's freshman year. But when Six drove the forty-five minutes to play for San José the next year, her arrival in NCAL volleyball was bottom-fold news. Six got to focus on her game in the shadow of Green's precedent.

While the early days of Six's braid (shorter then than it is now) revitalized a minor hair trend across genders, it was a gif of junior-year Green that made the girls college-sports famous. The two-second snippet showed Green's shapely ass cheeks bouncing as she pancake dove onto the floor. Never mind that the play ultimately ended with Green losing the point in a failed block. In the mid 2010s, the internet was not lacking for bare butt imagery, let alone clothed butt gifs. Of course, an image is more than its most obvious feature. It was the unexpected shape and physicality of Green's ass between her skinny legs and skinny torso, the intensity of her expression in profile, her high ponytail swirling in a perfect circle above her skull. Everyone saw something different in the moving image, but every casual internet browser felt a new attraction to Green. The endless loop of Green's slackened glutes sloshing in her seven-inch baby blue shorts was a revelation—in the renaissance of American volleyball, as a tipping point for trans girls in sports, and the upending of the stereotype of buttless Asian people.

Despite some lingering reticence, when Six was voted captain her junior year, she made something of a mascot out of herself. Her effortless charisma convinced the straightest of her teammates to paste glitter stamps on their cheeks for game days, a practice copied from the lady gymnasts. Meanwhile, as both players won conference titles and MVPs, they built a base of supporters who actually dragged their whole flesh to their games. Flying under the body paint of team spirit was a perfect cover if anyone needed it.

That spring, when San José and Lancaster were in the same bracket of the NCAL tournament, fans were eager for them both to advance to the semifinal so Six and Green could finally play against each other. When Green (@everyourgreen, 27k followers) watched game tape of Six (@sixsosweet, 18k followers) with her team, they had already followed each other for months. Dude, did you know there's another one of you out there?!

Six had considered DMing her but didn't want to force it. That Green also existed in the world at the same time as her and the league brought them to this same match was destiny enough.

After failing to qualify for the tournament in Six's freshman and sophomore years, San José was the Cinderella team facing off against Lancaster, the three-time defending champs. That morning, Green was particularly fastidious about putting herself together. Before their first match, Green wanted Six to see her as a girl who looked hot in person, not just in that gif that made her bubbly behind the prettiest thing on a screen. Her desire was neither erotic nor competitive. At this point in their lives, Green's edge in followers meant so little to her. She was just thrilled to have signed her first pro contract just weeks ago. Despite her family loving the sport, her parents had never wanted her to pursue it and nobody had expected her to actually take it to six figures. Now in the ladies' room, she angled her chin upward to see the inflamed electrolysis bumps drawing attention she didn't want to her upper lip. Her face wasn't always godly perfection. Green's pre-game playlist was so loud, she didn't hear the sound of Six's nervous pee. When the only person in San José's red and orange who could possibly be in there with her emerged from a stall, she quickly backed away from the mirror.

Six only saw Green washing her hands but realizing what was about to happen made her dizzy. That was her body, her ponytail in a baby blue scrunchie color-matched to her own warm-up set.

Green met Six's eyes in the mirror.

Six swallowed. As ever, she would be normal. Hey! I'm Six.

Green turned off the faucet. Hi. I'm Green.

Six blushed as she pumped soap into her hands. The average-heighted dispenser sink prompted her to crouch down a bit; she hoped it didn't look patronizing. It's nice to meet you. Finally, she said, smiling. Green was so gorgeous, so, so gorgeous in person.

Reaching behind Six to grab a paper towel, Green took in her impressive silhouette glistening in polyester, as if she didn't play with boys her height every day. Same. I'm so glad we're not alone. It sounded trite but she meant it.

When Six turned off her faucet, Green offered a towel and now they had to look at each other directly. Six might've drooled she felt so slack with gushy awe at Green's face, her body, her aura, the way she draped one leg demurely in front of the other, the way she extended the sensuous shape of her jaw forward as she looked inevitably up at Six.

When Six took the towel, somehow her fingers met Green's and Green surprisingly tingled at the sensation. Her knees could've collapsed onto the linoleum. She wasn't sure if this was eros or something else.

Leaving the bathroom, they parted ways before meeting again on the court.

The next day, Six opened her Instagraph to see a message from Green: I'm so glad to have finally met you. Congrats on winning yesterday! Can't believe you broke our winning streak but you were incredible. Can we stay in touch?

She might have ghosted had this happened her freshman year, but now that she'd taught the boys about glitter stamps and open communication, she was ready. On their first video call, she was less nervous now that they'd broken the ice. When she found out Green was relocating to Santa Cruz in a few months, she let her genuine excitement show and from there, their friendship became easy to grow. Green drove to San José when she wasn't traveling, and Six drove to Santa Cruz when she didn't have volleyball or class. That first year was exceptionally romantic. But early on, they decided that feeling probably wasn't sexual but something even more carnal, like a lifetime deprived of cultural representation. So they acknowledged the magnetic pull they felt to each other and chose friendship. The sexual tension broke and platonic tenderness took its place: little knee slaps here, brief snuggles there. They talked often about all the weird ways commentators and fans directed their curiosity toward them. They realized how alone they'd felt on their own teams and so, chose reliable companionship over fickle romance. Before moving to Italy for her first team camp, Six moved out of her apartment in San José and drove forty-five minutes to stay with Green for their first three-week summer. It was the radiant kiss-off to celebrate their first year of friendship.

But years later, their friendship had evolved. Six broached her feelings because she knew that she could no longer text her best friend like they were just friends. And Green was relieved. She hadn't wanted to risk unraveling what trust they had built together. On a dry sunny day on Green's balcony that summer, they recalled fondly that first year of knowing each other. Green agreed to Six's emphatic commitment to always return to that foundation, regardless of what would happen next. Part of her knew it was a faulty premise, though. If time wasn't linear, it could never really circle back on itself, but only appear to as it spiraled on.

All the while, their fanbases grew worldwide. Sonus recruited both Six and Green as sponsored stars to help launch its inaugural tournament in 2020. When Six and Green both made it to the final, Sonus compiled a fluff piece showing Green's ass-bounce gif, their most spectacular plays in slo-mo, and studio B-roll of two of its biggest stars posing atop pedestals.

It was a tough match. Every tension echoed around the empty stadium. When Regalado won, Six cried openly, her furrowed face conveying distraughtness, but her cheeks wide and legible to the camera. The best actors would appreciate her natural talent for conveying emotion on-screen. She made distraughtness look so aesthetically pleasing. When the two teams shook hands beneath the net, Green interrupted the procession and reached beneath the net to hug her girlfriend. Six sobbed even harder. She had wanted to win her last game with La Spezia so badly. Green wasn't even thinking of the cameras. She just held on to Six's wrists and, through the net, kissed her. That the pandemic had vacated live fans from the arena only made the soft earnestness of the gesture feel more intimate to the millions of at-home viewers, breathless worldwide.

Ugh! Look at them! Sonus's appointed color commentator Tanner exclaimed on the video that circulated the globe.

Stripped of its following sentences, Tanner's *Ugh!* could sound like affection or disdain, impatience or empathetic agony, or conveniently, any of these emotions at once. Regardless of whatever viewers projected onto the phatic utterance, one couldn't not hear the erotic pleasure in Tanner's voice. Tanner followed the sound with a narrative that made Six and Green's journey to that kiss satisfyingly relatable: "Like Romeo and Juliet. Or, Juliet and Juliet. Listen, Rudy, there was no way they could both leave this match thrilled. That's not how sport works. But these players from opposing teams have been friends since they first played each other in college and have been dating for over a season now. Beyond love, what we're witnessing right now on the court is a deep respect for each other."

The moment replayed on the sports network's evening recap and then, the next morning on its parent news channel's morning talk show. The hosts cooed atop Tanner's *Ugh!* with their own simpering wonder at all the affect bursting from the scene. The release of tears! The tender embrace! The fishbowl of nearby players patiently admiring their teammate and opponent, and the jumbotron creating a double portrait. Just look. The famed power couple just being a couple after a grueling five-set match.

It took only an hour for multiple platforms to track millions of views and Green's agent Yemma to call Six's agent Brent. They called Green and Six together in what would become the first of many four-way calls. They were a super team now. Yemma explained how this moment met her criteria for "viral." It wasn't the engagement stats but the revelation of new entry points toward infatuation. Viral moments reached vector viewers and taught them how to feel and bring the phone closer to their face. Six and Green's kiss was a beacon for romance and optimism in lonely, socially distanced times. If they could keep it together, maybe there was still hope.

###

I can't believe someone let a jungle Asian like Green pollute our noble sport. A faggot like Six is worthy because of his talent but

Seeing them kiss at the net awoke my flight response.

@bobababe59 is a troll, only faux-conscious, self-hating Asian people use the term "jungle Asian"

And then I froze. And ever since, I've been fawning.

Six, bro, your shoulders are amazing! That has to be part protein powder. What's your dose? Haha

How can they be dudes who are women who are lesbians who are into dudes and play on the men's team?

Green is of pure Japanese stock, I hear her family descended from the Yamata dynasty. Can't you tell from her glowing porcelain skin and almond eyes and sleek black hair?

Six, if you ever need a shoulder to cry on, I'm 6'4"!

That unruly voluptuous mess on Six's head is worthy of a red card.

And if fawning over them is a trauma response, they can traumatize me forever

So like, do they only have sex when they're in the same city three weeks a year?

If I had a girlfriend like Green, I'd be broke treating her so good

I'm pretty sure Green's ace and they're open and Six is a little slut

Six, you are so brave to display such profound emotion so openly on such a stage!

Isn't Six hooking up with Curtis?

The way Six can just lean on his partner after such a tough loss. Now that's love!

It's *her* partner! Green is *her* *girl*friend!

So doping isn't allowed but surgically or chemically altered men with nefarious gender schemes are? Reverse sexism must be stopped!

If these girls didn't have testosterone privilege, where did the muscle definition in Green's calves come from? Or those perfect veins in Six's biceps? Show me a woman who looks like they do.

Would people be half as interested in Six and Green if they weren't trans women? They just seem like basic bitch athletes with no star quality to me

Can we talk about Six's awful sportsmanship? Cry in the locker room, you sore loser

How can two sick people play volleyball so good?

@transaretrans if you're such an expert in charisma why don't you show us your face!?

Kinda funny to think about how we wouldn't be here

if Green hadn't bought her and Six those followers in 2015. Mother had a plan!

Fucking perverts! They oughta be slapped and whipped senseless! I could just smack their perky fat asses and tie these sickos by their powerful little wrists and choke their dainty little necks! Fuck!

###

Every platform marketed a purpose. They supposedly talked shop on Stack, watched each other play games on Discard, solicited advice on Seddit, offered unsolicited opinions on Flitter, shot elaborate films for TikTak, brand infinitum. People had something to say about Six and Green everywhere.

###

Green (@everyourgreen, 726k followers) scrolled through the latest practice clips Yemma had sent her. Lying on her emerald couch at home, Green checked her feed to remind herself where she was in her pattern. She posted in thematic cycles of four so that the distinct image types cascaded in a diagonal across her Instagraph profile.

Three posts ago, Green had shared a three-second video of her placing her left hand on left hip, right hand on right hip, bending at the knees, and rocking her pelvis side to side while she lip-synced the words "But won't you take me baby?" On *baby*, she swirled her ponytail around, her hair flashing in front of the camera lens before the video looped again. Her abridged take on the "Take Me!" challenge left viewers wanting more instead of criticizing Green's untrained dancing.

###

Look at those legs and tell me that's not a woman

Okay but Green has gotten so much better at dancing than she used to be!

Anyone else think it's toxic how she claims to be bad at social media?

I'll take you, you naughty girl @everyourgreen

What a bad dyke, she makes women look bad by playing into the male gaze like this, this is why trans women aren't good for feminism

Didn't Green detransition for a bit four years ago?

Alrighty #TeamSupaGreen, can everyone send this video to five of your friends and ask them to follow @everyourgreen and @TeamSupaGreen? We're so close to catching up to Six!

No homo but I'm a little hard for that bubble butt

This girl is clearly a pro. She's definitely manipulating her fans with that classic sales technique: Underpromise, overdeliver.

So you're saying if she was fat and didn't shave, she wouldn't be a woman? @tim3290

No @tim3290 she's been a lady for over a decade.

Well Green is trans so @spikycity isn't that straight

Finally, two famous Asian women who aren't dating white men!

I thought she went off estrogen because her doctor

Don't try to corner me @henryhits, it's the way she uses her legs. Only a woman could know how to use her legs, not their size or shape or texture, like that.

@transaretrans whatever regimen she did or didn't take, she never detransitioned.

Did you and Six break up? I heard she seduced her roommate at an away game

No way this took her 15 takes, I bet it was 3, she's so gifted

Ilysm can i take you pls @everyourgreen? Or take ME!

Green is a woman, you're still straight, relax @spikycity. But if you wanna be sure, DM me

###

Six helped Green learn choreo when they were together on holiday. Just another of Six's natural talents, which Green had to admit made her the more obvious fit for the collab with that ballerina. During the season, Green enlisted her teammate Ricky, who liked to dance but had no intentions of participating in the online record of this atemporal flash mob. It was a shame because at a full ten inches taller than Green, he would've made their videos so funny. Ricky was already planning for his own retirement. In three seasons, he would go back to school and become a nurse. He lived so frugally, as if Regalado didn't pay him half a million a year.

After "Take Me!" was an action shot accompanied by her usual caption contest. Yemma's team sent Green the top ten, and Green reposted her five favorites. Once, Green complained to Yemma about how Six didn't have to work as hard to boost her own engagement. Yemma gave her such a pitying look, she never complained about it again. Everyone had to work hard at different things, she told herself.

Green's latest post two days ago was a minute-long clip she'd filmed of her setting herself a volleyball while balancing in a V-sit, knees bent and feet flexed stiff. As she tapped the ball from the tips of her fingers and eyed its short flight just above her head, she talked about how the exercise was an easy way to build hand-eye coordination and reflexes while keeping her core strong and agile.

For today's post, Green pulled between her fingers a photo of an off-court outfit-of-the-day and began toggling the warmth and saturation filters to look more vibrant. The belt tied around the A-line wool coat and the angle of her legs, one stepping in front of the other, gave the impression of curves that every other photo on her grid revealed weren't there.

A vocal minority of the trans femme contingent of her fanbase saw through her tricks and loved her for it. They emulated her in their own posts, asked Green where she had bought that dress, whether it was bad for athletes to wear heels on off days. It probably wasn't the best, but they were more than athletes, Green would respond. They were women.

As a child, Green would stand and make herself look longer and taller than she already was, especially for a Japanese boy. One of her most womanly tells. An auntie would pinch her teenage ribs with incredulity. Now that you're tall, you have to keep eating so you get wide too, she would say whenever she saw Green. Green came out the next month. Self-consciously, Green would eat but the food just disappeared. To develop the lean muscle required for her profession, she had to understand her body better. She learned to feed her inner muscle girl who lifts for strength.

She always knew she was beautiful. She had convinced herself of it so long ago that when the public caught on, she was a buffed and polished surface ready to shine the light back. But still, when she first joined Instagraph a decade ago, she would spend an hour agonizing over a draft post. When fully nauseous from self-induced decision fatigue, she'd finally tap "Post" and toss her phone away. She never thought she'd become famous. Now that she was, she knew how much it cost. She navigated Instagraph's latest interface with a pleasant emptiness. She made decisive adjustments and pushed her little photos to her followers' phones with barely a twitch to interrupt her inert neck. This was work. The caption read: 16 days till the @Sonus Tournament!

Everything got easier with time.

She closed the app. She'd already liked and commented on the posts of the girls she hoped to be friends with. She'd return in half an hour to like her own comments and reshares, parsing the select reply or reshare of a reshare. She knew all the dizzying self-referentiality looked desperate but as far as Green could see on her feed, everyone was very desperate. Any whiner either became hypocritical through performative self-righteousness or simply had nothing of their own to contribute.

The only antidote was to redirect attention back to herself so her public image was so complete, it could never be contaminated. Green and Six had jobs that all but required them to hire teams who encouraged them to not be ashamed about it, who told them how to strategize, who made their strategies seem like the only way forward in such difficult, uncertain, unprecedented times. Regalado had given all its players basic media training, but Yemma had helped Green monetize herself. And Yemma cost money. Green was a setter, a gamemaker. She made split-second decisions with relentless precision. But she couldn't orchestrate her own fame by methodically accumulating points. To win, Green would keep throwing variations of her image at the feed till it reached the right eyes.

###

The first topic of tonight's *Six & Green* was managing jealousy. How did they both manage swarms of adoring fans and hot teammates while trusting in each other? The set locations of the episode were a neighborhood in Denver, where Green walked with her phone in her outstretched arm, and a luxurious bathroom in a Lublin apartment, where Six relaxed beneath bubbles in her tub. In New York, Guthrie watched on their computer on the floor in front of their couch, hoping that Green was up to the multitask. As Green walked confidently down hilly streets, Six smiled back as steady as ever, her reassurance as much for herself as for Green.

Here's how tonight's inspired viewers called it:

Green, if I hired a private chef and gave you an apron, would you give up volleyball and serve me dinner every night?

Why do y'all hog so much space in the trans community?

Like leave it to folks who actually risk something to leave the house and be trans.

Imagine being 6'1" and having a size difference kink and not having a giantess like Six to indulge you. Oh wait that's me.

What are they supposed to do after they retire? Nobody's gonna let them coach volleyball or run clinics. Not with minors!

Makes sense that Green's freeballing COVIS since Asia gave it to us in the first place.

I feel like if Green's telling Six how reassuring she is, it probably means Six makes her super anxious.

I wish Six would tell us what was really going on inside her head. She's so mysterious.

Um, Green is wearing a dress, is that not enough of a risk for you?

And all the best college teams are state schools and no state could

Also, imagine getting to have her proprioception 24/7

Sign up for @SixGreenSpike Clinic! Coming to 15 cities this summer!

I consider myself a pretty open-minded person but ever since that Dulce partnership, I haven't been able to look at Six the same way. I never saw you as someone who would willingly take jobs from real women.

Pardon the pun but Six seems a little cocky. I mean, Green plays on the same team as Ricky.

If anything this episode makes me think Six sleeps with her groupies when she's bored.

No, I mean, imagine being a lady like Six in that tub and getting to look down and see that, all wet.

@SixGreenSpike is a scam! @Instagraph #TeamSupa-Green report them!

Even if Green is a gold star trans lesbian, I'd judge her for not being at least a little attracted to him.

Six used to be a regular on the forums but when she got famous, [1/x]

Let's be honest, they're not worried about dying, they're worried about missing work. Love how they stay relatable

she got her heart broken by someone pretending to be a friend but really just wanted to sleep with her. [2/x]

So you people should try to have some respect for her privacy [3/x]

Exactly @SixSweeties, that's why I want to be inside Six's mind. To know what else is going on in that beautiful head of hers. To know what she thinks and feels.

I feel like girls who desired so intensely to become women who love women probably know more about being women than girls who were always going to become women

Green does cross train, have you not seen any of her videos @tim3290? Or the episode where she held a plank for seventeen minutes straight?

Do you ever think about how your feed tells you what to think?

It's true, even though Green may seem cold and stiff, at least what you see is what you get. Six is so expressive, but I feel like she's always keeping just a little bit to herself! It's not fair that Green gets to know what she's really like.

I try to teach this hell site to not show me the people who think girls like us should just die but I think the algorithm wants me to see them so I get mad and keep spiral scrolling.

###

Toward the end, people started trickling out and before it looked embarrassing, they signed off. Green buzzed her lips and blew nervous breath into her eyeballs. She veered to the riverside path just ahead as Six called her back.

Hey, babe! Six said needlessly, almost needily, her voice disembodied from the image of her pale blue ceiling as she toweled off.

Sixy! Hi!

How'd you feel? Beanie, you did so good!

Aw, thanks. That was stressful! Oh wow, Guthrie says I did great too.

It's true. I don't think I could handle that multitasking.

You'd have been better at it than me!

Hey, come on, but Guthrie thought you should've done it.

Why me, do you think?

I don't know. We should ask!

Next week, think we'll still do the show from our sides of the bed?

Six giggled in delight, her face now bouncing in front of a whirring apartment. The thought of seeing her Green after so many months apart . . .

We'll see, I guess, Six said, her image finally stable, her

body in a sweatsuit cloud of lime green. I'm excited to see Curtis and Henry too.

Their closest friends in the league were such sweet boys.

Same, Green said. Did you catch today's comments at all?

Not really, you know I can't really keep track of them. Why, what'd you see?

I don't know, just felt like more trolls than usual to me, saying how we're not even women. It did feel like more of it was coming after me.

Really? Six asked.

People kept saying I should just become an actual trans woman and that I'm a danger to public safety.

That's just people being horny and not knowing it so they're mad about it, Six said. They had talked about this before. But still, I'm sorry that you caught all that, bean. How did you pay attention to all of it?

I guess something about having to keep track of my route and the score all at once also kept my brain on alert for the comments? I wish I hadn't seen it, she lied.

Six's wet hair glistened behind her as she walked. Once they had reached this part of a conversation flow, it was easiest to stay in it. You're such a girl, Six said, caring what these losers and bots think about us.

Green still looked sad. I guess it just reminds me that people are so simple-minded. Like I'm the femme girl and you're the butch girl but like, I'm sorry, I don't mean to put you back into what the internet thinks. Does it not bother you?

Not really. I feel like I can't take what these randos say

seriously. At the end of the day, they showed up to our show, and the ones who harass us are a minority compared to the thousands who are excited to just tune in and don't comment at all.

You're right, sweetie, Green said, though her eyes seemed unconvinced.

Every week, we get the same questions about hormones and league rules and how we're fake women. And Yemma and Brent tell us we don't have to explain anything to these people again. We say it once a year. The league made their statement six years ago. All of this is searchable information. People are just lazy and terrible.

Green brushed a loose thread of hair behind her ear, where it blew free in the breeze.

I can't wait to see you next week, lady, Green said. The sentiment was as true and obvious as calling her woman-girlfriend lady, and yet, Green didn't know what else to say. The comments floating upstream still played in her mind.

Same! It's been months! I miss you, bean.

Miss you too! For Six and Green, transness could never be an abstraction about selfhood or spirituality. It could only ever be about gonads and hemoglobin counts. For over half a decade, this fixation had given them an uncontested corner of trans discourse they'd never wanted. Six could see how it was wearing on Green. And while debriefing was genuinely comforting, they hadn't actually done any new work on just them. Six squinted into the sun as she reminisced on the last weekend they had spent together. More than sharing the same air hand in hand, they'd been able to really talk. Privately. It was nearly five months ago. The back half of the season always felt like an interminable rally.

Walking back to her apartment, Green worried that all this negative engagement might limit growing their platforms or securing new sponsorships. She knew she couldn't ask Six for reassurance. Six would be nice about it but she'd also be alarmed that her girlfriend cared so much about their relationship's potential for clout.

###

Green (#19, 6'1", 159 lbs.) shook her head. Her damp ponytail plopped against her forehead as she bent at the hips, her hands massaging her gelatinous quads.

Oliver blew the whistle.

Green crouched to receive. She had to keep it together. This was Regalado's arena, the professional home of her entire career. But she couldn't relax here. She eyed the second-string setter Walt watching her not watch the ball hurtling her way. Her eyes darted back to the ball but she overcorrected and made contact a split second too early, making it impossible for Ken to give it a real set. Ricky swung but spiked it into the net.

Easy, Green! You with us today? Oliver called.

Green eyed Walt and felt the space behind her eyes throb again. Oliver didn't ask her if she wanted Walt to sub in for her but she imagined it anyway.

Yep! She knew better than to explain her stiff elbows. It'd just make her sound insecure, and to keep her spot, she had to make like a man and just move on. Starters needed coaching too, but they couldn't let a benchwarmer sniffing for a vulnerability catch it.

She slapped her thighs. She hadn't slept much after yesterday's live but she was a pro. She buzzed the tension out of her lips and eyed the next serve. Thankfully, someone else caught the first touch and passed it her way so she could perform her primary function: setting. She skittered two steps to her right and sparkled her fingers in a perfect pass to Ken, who spiked it between the block.

That's it, Oliver said. That's it! Need me to remind you every serve that you're playing? He could've softened the chide with sass, but his tone conveyed a threat. From her first season, she had asked to be treated just like any of the boys. But it was an impossible request and she would always wonder if he was tougher on her, or if the threats he made to the boys stressed them out or just rolled off because, well, boys. Walt couldn't carry a real game on his own but she couldn't get complacent.

She rejoined the starters for the post-rally huddle. Even boys just had to co-regulate after each point. If they wanted to win, they had to gather close to congratulate each other, strategize, and trash-talk an opponent, all while gently patting each other's hips and butts and low backs before sending each other back to their positions. It wasn't a huddle without the touch. From birth until death, people looked for people they could touch and be touched by comfortably. Spectator sports were invented so lonely people could at least watch other people touch each other.

But the viewers watching whom Green touched and was touched by wouldn't see much. When she regrouped with the boys, she didn't even grumble about Oliver. She just nodded and *mhm*ed while remembering the feeling of Six's hands cradling her neck, her breath on her ear, the way they elbowed and hipped each other all day when they were together. If a girl couldn't participate in the boys' huddle haptics, she could still daydream.

At least until she had to set. She had to tell herself her headache wasn't worsening, that Oliver hadn't just made her more hypervigilant, he'd made her better. If everyone had to distinguish between her intuition and femininized paranoia, they'd feel oversensitive too. She'd signed up for this existential dissonance but the consent she gave at thirteen could not have been sufficiently informed.

And so, for the rest of the practice, she made plays like a male genius and smiled like a soccer mom. She had to show Walt that he could never do what she could. It wasn't fair that Green's direct alternate was the only other Asian person on the team. Nor was it fair that Walt wouldn't soon get the reps that would teach his body to make the surest play faster. But sports weren't fair and Green's body already knew exactly how to touch the ball each time.

###

Just a couple of hours later it was already the next morning for Six (@sixsosweet, 883k followers). On their morning call, Green had been nervous about practicing on so little sleep, but at least she would be starting regardless. Pete hadn't rearranged the scrimmage lineups at all last practice. She was realizing that no matter how brutally she blocked, she still wouldn't start. It was crushing.

With a couple hours before her own practice, Six curled her neck around her phone, where little headlines and little takes on the headlines floated up her screen. A career of middle blocking had made the rhythms of jumping and stuffing at the net automatic. But even after a decade of fame, the gestures required to use her phone still felt clunky. Scrolling past the latest evidence in the president's corrupt dealings, Six remembered how unfathomable it was that she got to play sports while the world continued to splatter from its seams. He had made a big fuss on his Flitter about the importance of protecting their country, all while signing laws protecting pharmaceutical companies' patents over the vaccine and incentivizing airlines to shuttle people and their germs back and forth across his empire's made-up borders. And Six was a frequent flier. Six wasn't deluded that her job was a burden of altruism. She saw how traveling the world only to go numb on a bench still turned gears in an economy that was moving on from the pandemic. It was over, they insisted. Hundreds of people counted on the trickles they collected of her team's profits.

She had signed only a one-year contract with Czwartek and even though she'd hardly played this season, she knew she wanted to stay. And while they'd said they wanted to commit to her long-term development with the team, she knew nothing was guaranteed. Two teams had been dissolved in the past year, releasing a couple dozen players into a league already backlogged with fresh twenty-year-olds looking for a job. Six knew she had to start.

She'd learned from Green that staying active online was a way for her to indirectly keep making her case. From her first game on Czwartek's bench, she set out to use her image to remind her team's management whom they spent so much money on to sit on a stationary bike every weekend. When she reached 77 inches at 16 years old, she couldn't tell if people stared at her open-mouthed because she was hot or just tall. But as her jaw sharpened, she learned how to wield the power of having a face like a knife. When she made Dulce & Gabbano look hot, she also made Czwartek look hot. A tap on Six's profile boosted the Czwartek brand and, indirectly, the team merch store. Teams had been hurting for ticket sales all season. But with the upcoming Sonus Tournament already sold out, Six had plays to make.

She exited out of the news and found the post Clara had tagged her in. She commented, "So fun, Clara! Let's play volleyball next time," and shared the clip of them waltzing together to her story.

Like Green, she had a consistent pattern for her main feed: Six fed a photo through an app that tiled it three-by-three. Across the nine snippets, shared over the course of a few days, she'd post random musings and questions. Her fans reveled in watching the composite image reveal itself. People were so sad.

She found the next image in her queue, a tile of her padded left knee. She wrote, "Being alive is tiring! Like having to wake up and brush my crusty teeth and put on clothes and ingest food? Exhausting. How are y'all hanging in?" She read it over for typos and posted it. Before the photo finished rendering, she saw a flurry of hearts flashing frantically in the corner.

###

Are you not gonna say anything about the vaccine patent? The rest of us want to be safe too!

I've never seen an athlete so ungraceful, it really doesn't matter what she posts huh

It's so sad how Six is so obviously scared of being perceived.

Why don't they wear those tiny leotards for games??

With that height and those big eyes, I just know a red-blooded American soldier raped his mom during the war.

Those calves. So thick yet so slender, yum

Not all Asians are monolidded @bobababe59.

Aww Six, I feel like you're really enjoying yourself, maybe you should quit volleyball and join the ballet

Six, it's okay, you can be yourself with us. We're a safe space, you don't have to be so performative.

The virus won't kill me but this video of Six dancing in a racer back tank top might

So Six got double eyelid surgery?

Six looks good but not as good as Green did in that Take Me dance.

It's okay Six, not all of us could ever look like a real girl, your womanhood is still important!

Remember how Clara posted that meme of the white hand and Black hand shaking hands last summer? And now Six is like, yeah, it's fine, I'll do it for the money.

Yeah fuck Six, she may be the most talented blocker on the circuit but she's spineless!

Which lane do you mean @transaretrans? Cause she's a beautiful dancer and volleyball player and transvestite woman and you're stuck in traffic! Ha!

The internet already decided Six is hotter, stop trying to fight destiny

Yeah at least Green is annoying because she's so earnest, not because she's too cool for us

Please Six, just marry me!! If not, just spike a ball into my face, please, I'll pay! I've got like, $27 in my bank account!

###

Sitting at the edge of her bed, Walt (Regalado #29, 6'3", 181 lbs.) scrolled through the forums searching for a soothing update before sleep. The first new post read:

Omg, I TOTALLY agree, it's so scary but I wish you all the courage to take this next step. You got this sis!

Walt rolled her eyes. Her. She. She looked down at her body, naked but for satin panties that did not become her. She carried muscle, but her slackened abdominals looked more bloated than delicate. She thought of Green's body, already so womanly, both more toned and supple in relaxation than Walt could ever achieve with maximum exertion. This wasn't just pro sports dysmorphia—it was dysphoria. And Green's sets—always so precise, yet somehow, her spikes had the brute force of the best opposites. She thought of Green and her hot girlfriend Six and their combined 1.6 million followers and Green's starting place on the lineup and felt an envy of not *not* erotic intensity. The way Green played up being trans, the way she accentuated her Asianness. Walt was Asian too. Walt was trans too. She just wasn't out yet. Green lived in a sun-kissed penthouse in downtown Santa Cruz. Walt lived in a gloomy studio in the suburbs and in the trans closet of society's making. Even on these trans girl forums, she lurked but never posted, never asked her own questions or shared her own updates.

Walt (@waltsetset, 23k followers) looked at her public profile, full of the same basic content that Green posted: game photos, practice clips, food posts. But she was effectively irrelevant. It wasn't random that Green had so many more fans than her. Green was a unicorn. A token. Online, Walt just looked like another sports dude.

The algorithm didn't want trans people to succeed online, but Six and Green had outmaneuvered. Green and Six had become famous in an entirely different era of internet history. Ten years ago, if a video banked ten million views in a week, a little article republished it with a generic play-by-play sandwiched by a bland lede and canned punchline. The clickbait era of news ping-ponged the same bits into profit oblivion. Walt had first heard about Six and Green from one such article and had been horrified by the accompanying journalism: Why were those beautiful boys calling themselves girls?

These days, millions of videos got millions of views each day, and Walt was still working through her shame. The playing field hadn't been leveled. It had merely widened into a mêlée, no teams, just countless players moshing and mashing each other over control of the attention ball. Everyone was famous and no one was. Six and Green had to do more to make the news but being grandfathered in as internet celebrities made it an easier serve. Green should've been a role model for Walt, but seeing the couple's follower counts grow since starting that ridiculous weekly live show only scared her. What if Walt tried to enter the mess and was mauled alive by transphobe trolls? Worse, what if she posted a video of her doing a girly little dance and nobody watched it?

Walt's neck tensed as she scrolled through her own feed, reading captions that didn't sound like either a man or a woman wrote them, especially not beneath her mannish-looking photos. She wanted to grow her hair out, but then she would have to suffer through that awful awkward length that lasted years before finally looking hot. What would she do with it for volleyball? Put it up in a heinous headband until it could be collected in a tiny tuft of a ponytail? Or worse, something the coaches would call a man bun? And if she did hitch her career on Green's trans wagon, the team still wouldn't follow her back. Everyone respected Green, but they would view Walt's artless mimicry as opportunistic at best. More likely, they would watch her gradual transition and wonder why she'd chosen to become an ugly woman when she could've just been a dude. Maybe the coaches would give her more playing time. Benching your second, less pretty girl on the boys' team would be transmisogyny.

Walt tapped to Regalado's latest video to find a clip to

post to her own page. She wanted an excerpt that didn't show Green in the background but she was inescapable. There was Green jogging, her silky black ponytail flowing like the wind. Walt huffed a few paces behind her, her mouth tight, her fists lumpy. There was Green, rolling her eyes and giggling at the camera like an anime girl. Walt mimicked the gesture alone in her bedroom. She told herself she was mocking Green but, obviously, she was emulating. How badly Walt wanted to be that girl, starting every game, drawing the crowd, the one management asked to give these asinine interviews about nothing, nothing at all, just so many nods and smiles and infuriatingly feminine flips of her perfect hair.

Who wouldn't be attracted to the effortless elegance emanating from the fastest twitching neck in the league? Whatever your gender, whatever your sexuality, whatever your internalized racial biases, one couldn't see Green shaking her legs between rallies and not want to fuck her, be fucked by her, and be her all at the same time.

Walt sighed. All clips of her led back to Green, that stunning specimen. She spliced a clip of her fist-bumping Green at the end of the day's scrimmage. On the sidelines, Walt was sweating needlessly from her chin—why the chin?—while Green just glowed splendidly preparing to receive. Walt didn't mean for the algorithm to drive the most devoted portion of Green's fanbase to Walt's page but she knew it would happen. Many of them would already have seen whatever clip Green had posted. But at least a few thousand would be delighted to stumble upon this random dude who didn't even start for Regalado but had physical contact with their crush. Through

Green's profile, fantasies splayed and sprayed out on the internet for anyone with a connection to witness. Walt imagined Green telling her, I always had a feeling that you were one of us, and hit the spray button on her phone.

###

SET

AS LONG-DISTANCE GIRLFRIENDS DO, SIX AND GREEN were converging across space time on SpaceTime before actually reuniting. Thankfully, their data plan bypassed their respective airports' overcrowded, low-speed Wi-Fi. Green had been in walking distance of her gate for an hour, while Six just cleared security.

You looked so effortlessly good in that video, babe. You make sweat look delicate, but also, so hot! Six looked conspiratorially around her, as if one of her fans might be nearby and think she was talking to them. I can't wait to kiss the sweat on your face.

Green didn't mention this latest video's twenty-four-hour view count, 116,000, the highest so far this season. Views were higher a year ago when much of the world had been on lockdown and everyone watched anything. And now, even as the virus kept spreading, so were vaccines and it was spring and people would rather go outside than look up Green's Instagraph (@everyourgreen, 743k followers).

Instead, she brought baby pink polished nails to her throat. Babe, I just can't wait till I can see your face. The anticipation made it even easier to be so sickeningly sweet to each other and every new piece of content their teams published was worth a thousand recaps.

Six was giving an inventory of her snacks when Green received a notification: "I can't believe @waltsetset gets to learn from @everyourgreen EVERY DAY. Like what a privilege to be able to set with THE BEST, you must be SO thankful Walt!!" Green swiped the notification up, blushing as she did with every nice comment she received.

Six didn't see the blush through Green's mask but she saw the smirk in her girlfriend's eyes as a familiar sign of a stray notification. She changed the subject. Isn't it weird how there's all this hype for this tournament and we're finally going to play for live fans again, but like, people are still dying?

Green responded, Do you mean from the pandemic specifically or from every structural inequality the pandemic is making worse?

Green! Six tried not to laugh as she pouted, trying to be serious, but also the urge to laugh was easier than taking Green's response seriously, or taking her own question seriously. Laughter maintained social distance.

What? Green responded, one hand held up as if balancing a platter. With only the above-titty body parts to express themselves, they deployed these emoji-esque gestures all the time.

Green! Six mimed the face-palm emoji.

What are we supposed to do? Quit our jobs and go out to do what? Protest? Complain about it to our fans? We saw what good that did last year.

That's not what I meant, Six said. It's just odd that our jobs get to continue through all this. We get to do what we love and we're paid well for it.

Yeah, and we only get to live like this for so much longer. We already lost half a season at the peak of our careers. Last year was cute for a little while, but we've gotta look out for us. Whether we like it or not, it's back to business. Green didn't mention how she played every game and just barely made more than Six, all because Czwartek was based in one of the biggest volleyball nations in the world. And Czwartek's existing roster of happy sponsors only made the team more appealing to new sponsors.

Six grimaced behind her mask, both at the grim reality of what Green had said and at her resignation. Last year had begun with fresh hope soon felled by a new viral pathogen. Then, the possibility of a slower way of life had been felled by austerity and denial of mass death. Six and Green had gone from that viral through-the-net kiss to hiding, to helping their elderly neighbors with errands, to livestreaming their funerals, from telling everyone to get out and march to wondering if it had meant anything. For a few months, they pretended to be normal people for the first time in a decade. Then, protests and promises to do better circled back to some uncanny mutation of where they had been before.

Six and Green felt the sullen sting in the return to their grueling team schedules. When it was confirmed the fall season would proceed, Green didn't question the pre-pre-season workout her coaches had sent. She got back in shape and Six got COVIS. While Six was still coughing, they filmed demo episodes of *Six & Green* and worked with Guthrie to enhance their on-screen chemistry. Before they could even interrogate how or why, they had escaped back to their detached bubble of celebrity.

Cycling through so much hope and disappointment left everyone on edge. If work was humiliating, at least anyone could lash out at anyone else in very important arguments online. Not that Six and Green were immune to this rhetorical logic. They could go from being saccharine to so sour sensitive so quickly. Volatility was the new rhythm in these unprecedented times. It wasn't just about winning. It was about good ethics! Six breathed. She was in an airport talking to her girlfriend through a phone, both of their mouths obscured, Green's raised eyebrow either a defiant provocation or a wonky camera angle. Green being right didn't address Six's question but now was not the time to have an argument, even if it needed to happen. Behind Green, the sun blistered at the reflective edges of brutalist airport design. Six softened seeing how the light made her partner squint.

I mean, we've always tossed balls around so randos can whoop themselves hoarse, Green said. It's a weird job.

Yeah, sorry, Six said, both genuinely apologetic and annoyed that she should feel that way. I wasn't trying to have a whole discussion about what we're doing with our lives.

It's okay, we're all an inch away from an existential crisis, Green said. She would prefer to pet Six's head, run her hands through her thick hair and let her fingers gently separate the tangles. Soon enough. She guessed Six's adorable mouth was a little slack but not even the tech companies could know. And then she heard the word *selfie* float through Six's EarPods.

Some *Six & Green* fans showed up! Wanna say hi?

Before Green could respond, Six was already rotating her arm around a couple of swooning teenagers.

Green's Live Grin appeared in record time. Had Six been looking, she would've recognized it even through the mask. Green waved animatedly from Six's palm-sized screen at the fans, dressed in dark gray sweats and brightly colored hoodies.

I'm on the phone with Green right now! Six said.

The fans' eyes looked at Green's blurry hand for barely a second before staring back up at all of Six's 79 inches and 204 pounds. Green lowered her hand and now her face appeared 2 inches tall and 1.5 inches wide nestled against Six's 11-inch hand.

You're even taller in real life, one of them said.

Dude, what's your spike height?

Oh, c'mon. Six brought herself closer to the fans so Green could watch the whole scene play out. You should meet James, he's literally 6'11".

Wait, can we?

Seriously, your spike height's probably, what, like 350? I'm still at 320 but hopefully I'll get there someday.

I'm sure you will, Six said. Mine's 357. But it's taken me years.

Oh Six, I'm about to board. There are my teammates, Green lied.

Are y'all coming to the tournament?

Six, I'll meet you in baggage claim? Green said.

Oh shit, sorry babe, yes of course, you land . . .

Just twenty minutes before you, Six.

That's right, safe flight, cupcake! Mwah!

And to top it off, it was Six who ended the call, the teenagers still fanbroing. Let them get their selfies, Green thought. She wasn't jealous of children. She was just impatient to see her girlfriend. If she'd been standing around, she'd be asked for autographs too. But she was tired. When boarding began, Green begrudgingly assumed her full height, six inches shorter than Six, and followed her teammates onto the runway.

###

Green regarded her nails, shining in cured Regalado magenta but cut impossibly short. You couldn't set if your nails blocked your fingertips. But after this tournament, the claws were coming back.

She was in her hotel room—Six's connecting flight had been delayed, so Green had gone ahead without her. She thought of Six's question before they'd been derailed by those fans. Maybe she could consider it more thoughtfully when she wasn't in a busy airport or thousands of miles in the sky. She'd maintained intense focus all season with only a cursory *Why* to propel her: if times were so uncertain, she would do everything she could to make the next shock less destabilizing. Yemma was setting up the next stage of Green's career but they all involved Green continuing to pass balls. When the blustering buffoon of a president had been reelected, Green wanted to join the demonstrations, but she was tired. So instead, she soaked in an Epsom salt bath, her phone on mute in the living room.

Tonight she was catching up on the day's news.

- With vaccinations widely available in the United States, infection rates held steady at 0.01 percent for the past month.
- The upcoming Sonus Tournament would be the first indoor sports event of its size open to the public since the pandemic, with safety protocols for both the athletes and audiences.
- A noted celebrity couple was divorcing, after a very public seventeen-year marriage.
- A popular cereal, whose sales had recently suffered, redesigned its logo, to much outrage.
- Three trans Asian American women were found murdered in a hotel room in Alpharetta. The suspect is on the loose.
- Two celebrities whose affair had dominated the tabloids nineteen years ago have gone viral

on social media with their re-kindled not-so-secret romance.

- Protestors in three major cities marched against newly implemented vaccine requirements, calling them socialist-authoritarian insults to their civil liberties.
- It has been one year since a noted actor died from COVIS.

Green's jaw sank. She flipped between images of Luke and Teddy making out on the deck of some boat and a stock photo of a hotel. Luke's goatee was gray but Teddy's body still looked nice, considering how pap photos made everyone look pallid. From news site time stamps, Green gathered the story had broken only twenty minutes ago. She tried to find more info about the victims but the police hadn't yet released their names. Her Flitter notifications were full of people asking if she'd seen the news.

Green you must be so devastated

Green do you feel in danger?

Green did you know these girls?

Green did you see the news?

Green why aren't you saying anything about this?

It took only a minute for her to find their names: Suzy Akhter, Clarisse Valdez, and Bea Tran. She whispered the names to herself. She saw the same collage of photos of three beautiful girls floating but couldn't take the images in. Was this real? Even without more detail, she knew this wasn't a coincidence. Green's rib cage sank against the hotel headboard and she began to type.

###

Six didn't receive Green's texts about the murders till she landed. She called her immediately. What the fuck? she said, as a greeting.

I know, Green said, her voice brittle.

I don't even, I'm so exhausted, I just got off a plane.

I know, Green said. I'm glad you're safe.

Do they know anything more about the victims?

I don't know. I'm so tired. Green began to cry.

I know, babe, I know, Six said, imbuing each "I know" with comfort and reassurance. How mindlessly she swept in.

Green wailed, I just can't, how am I supposed to sleep?

I know, Six said soothingly. She had to hang up to go through customs.

When Six got to the hotel, Green was waiting masked in the lobby. When they hugged, they both began crying again. Six choked on her mask as she tried to gulp down her shock at the news and the relief of being with her girlfriend. Before either could metabolize all the competing sensations, they had to separate. Anyone with a petty grudge could catch them breaking COVIS protocol. For three days, all players were supposed to isolate in their rooms unless on the court or eating outside. Weeping, Green squeezed Six tighter before darting up the elevator alone so they could SpaceTime from their separate rooms. At least, they had made it to the same time zone.

Green was still sobbing. And we have practice tomorrow.

Seeing Green's snot and splotch, Six's throat closed up, dry and raspy. I know.

Do you ever, like, this is one of those days where you just? Green gasped, her breathing shallow.

Beanie, Six said, her voice now even and placating. This is awful. I wish I could be with you.

They talked, or rather, sat with each other online for another seventeen minutes before Six crawled into the shower and Green crawled into bed. Maybe it would've been easier for Six to keep crying if they'd been in person. They had known the tournament protocol but it felt even more devastating that they were in the same town, the same building, and not even able to grieve together.

Somehow Six slept, her body completely exhausted from the travel and shock to keep her up any later. When she woke, she remembered immediately. They had been girls like her. They were girls nothing like her at all. This happened all too often. This happening was uniquely terrible. She patted concealer in the dark splotches beneath her eyes without having to see herself. Green had taught her well. A pat of highlighter across her eyelids and Six was done. She had hidden the jet lag from her face and made her inner turmoil invisible to the male gaze. She SpaceTimed Green.

You ready? Green said, turning from her laptop to look at Six on her phone. Czwartek had the first practice slot of the morning but Regalado wasn't scheduled till the afternoon.

Six swallowed the news down. Guess so.

You gonna kick Sam off the team, baby?

Six leaned her skull forward in response. She guessed they weren't talking about it. Maybe Green thought distraction was better. Mm, she said.

What's your game plan?

They ran through it again.

That's my girl! Smash his ugly face.

Six saw Green shift her focus back to her own mirror. What about you?

I'm just gonna respond to some of these comments, Green said, finally alluding to the murders but without acknowledging them. Then I'll toss some dumbbells around downstairs, nothing too heavy, just enough so lunch doesn't slow me down for practice.

I'm still in shock, Six said. It's horrible.

I know, babe. It'll be okay. I'll let you finish getting ready.

So that was it. Six placed sunglasses over her eyes and blew a kiss goodbye. She took the sunglasses off and did some dissociated jumping jacks and burpees. She then turned to that awfully trans activity of regarding her full-length figure in the sliding closet door mirror. Her arm veins already protruded, even though she'd hadn't exerted herself. Would somebody try to kill her? As she turned to the side, she kind of looked like a man to herself, something she could never admit in public. But then she flipped her hair and saw her half-finished braid cascade its untamed bottom from one shoulder to the other. She knew her figure didn't make her a boy, but she wasn't sure if it would protect her either. She felt a novel resentment for what she would soon force herself to do.

I'm a girl playing boy sports, she told herself. I'm a killer. She'd said these words before. She felt sick.

Six gathered the jacket she'd planned to wear before the news. The lime green pleather sporty trench was mostly stiff wrinkles and air. It felt too bright today, but lime green had been one of her signature colors since before she met Green and Brent had made sure she sustained it in developing her brand. Today, her heart sunken and mind vacant, her brand identity was there to sustain her. Whatever she felt, she had to work or otherwise be in breach of her contract. In this stiff jacket, she could only stand with conviction. She put the sunglasses back on.

On the mercifully silent bus ride, Six thought through her *Whys*. She had to use this tournament to remind Czwartek she wasn't an older player to let age off a team, but an expensive poach at the height of her powers. She had to make sure her next contract guaranteed her starting.

At the start of the season, Six was told her unanticipated benching days would be temporary. They just wanted to ease her into the team rhythm and, come early winter, she'd be up and Sam would be in the back. She couldn't see how her coaches had watched her start for her previous team, La Spezia, and then left her stuck on a fold-out chair. Some people might say Sam was bigger (212 lbs.), taller (6'8"), faster, more precise. Some days, she'd be one of them, especially since contracting the virus last year. But at 27, she knew her value add wasn't physical potential but somatic intuition. She could get the other six bros to empathize with each other so well that their flow became impossible to derail. At least, before she joined Czwartek.

With the non-starters rotating configurations to emulate every opponent, no combination of players could get used to each other. The starters gelled fine but they had clear vulnerabilities. Six needed to show Pete and the rest of the team how she could help build team intuition. It was more than hand signals. There are energetically mysterious, astrally resonant planes through which a team could find flow! It was more than breath. It was feeling. It was the Six-th sense.

La Spezia setter Luca had coined the term, not her. Six should've mentioned it from day one at Czwartek, but she had been patient. But she was out of time and could not let some far-off murders derail her. After crinkling her coat in her locker, Six took in the beautiful arena. The court was bordered by waist-height flat screen TVs that would flash the logo of their maker and sponsor, Sonus, among half a dozen other advertisers. The field of play shone in muted shades of teal and orange. Six tested the spring of the court with soft knees. If age had given her any wisdom, it was the sensitivity to tell it was sprung and wooden, not concrete.

Six started warming up a ball between her fingers and eyed her fellow benchwarmers dragging their bodies across foam rollers. All the starters still dawdled in the locker room. Had she erred by not sticking with them? Then Alan, the still-nervous newbie, emerged. Here was the first target of her plan. Six would not be nervous like Alan.

Alan, hey!

Hey?

Pepper with me?

Oh, uh sure!

Alan eyed her with hesitant-looking wrists. She passed him the ball and reflexively, his forearms bound together and he bumped the ball nice and high.

Six didn't look to see Pete watching them, his face impassive. Nor did she look at Igor, who walked in with his own spiked foam roller under his armpit. She just followed the ball and let her own reflexes take over.

Hey Six, can you help me practice block out again?

Six caught the ball, caught off guard by Alan's direct question. Really? she thought. On the one hand, the opening match was in four days and the rookie still didn't have it. On the other, it was like he was somehow in on her plan.

Sure! Six said. She did some high knees and butt kicks in place, feeling her ankles roll smoothly on and off the court. She tossed the ball to Alan and ducked under the opposite side of the net.

Did you need to warm up your approach at all?

Oh, uh, I meant, um. Alan looked sheepish. He looked to see if Pete could see him needing more help. Pete conferred with one of the assistant coaches over a binder. I meant, could you help with just blocking?

Oh! Sure! Absolutely. They couldn't really practice it without someone spiking an actual ball to his side but she went back to his side of the net anyway. So, what is it about blocking? Six tried, neither wanting to condescend nor be unhelpful.

Pete looked up from his binder and saw them, his face still blank. While more players warmed up, Sam was still out. Alan folded his timid wrists behind his back. Well, I feel like I'm always a little early or late and I'm not really sure how to time when to go up.

Self-awareness was better than hubris, Six thought. Well, first, let's start with tracking your opponent. She ducked back under the net. As I move, look only at my feet and try to mirror me. Six positioned herself just off of Alan and started bouncing between the balls of her feet, side to back to side to front and around.

She watched as he watched her ankles with deep concentration, his brown hair flopping just above his brow. Yet, his arms held the perfect amount of tension.

See how your timing is just a bit slow? Try spotting the patch of air just behind my body instead of looking at me directly.

Pete asked the rest of the team to start laps but left Alan and Six alone. When Six repeated the exercise, she made faster, more syncopated changes in direction. And Alan kept up better this time, his pelvis always angled toward Six even as his torso faced away. He did have many good instincts. But how had he gotten this far without this most fundamental skill being better cultivated? Six played outside once, that first week of college. Her coach had obviously recruited her as middle but wanted to see if she was versatile. She wasn't but she could at least hit.

So with tracking, you can't stare directly at your target the whole time, especially when you're tracking where your team is. Six wouldn't explicitly reference the Six-th sense, but she would describe it to him. She'd had all season to articulate what the starters weren't doing enough. Six crossed back beneath the net. Now let's say I'm your middle.

Grapevines! Pete called.

Six had to speed it up. So you wanna use your peripheral vision. You wanna listen to where we're stepping relative to you. But you also want to activate a more general sensory awareness. Put your hand on my chest?

Alan looked at her blankly and extended a delicate hand just in front of his own stomach.

Mind if I? Six asked.

Uh, sure, Alan looked away. Sweet boy.

She took the back of his hand, soft and cool, and placed it a few inches below her throat. Now move with me.

She moved a bit slower, her hand still over his. He looked at his hand beneath hers, looked at her looking back at him, his neck suddenly stiff.

Don't look at me. Relax. Pretend the opposite team is setting something up.

As Alan eyed the other side of the court, Six released her hand and began moving once again in faster, more complex patterns. Alan's hand resting lightly on her sternum, they moved together. He was no longer a split-second behind her but changing direction at the same time and to the same degree as Six.

Now the other team digs the ball. Setter sets. And—

Alan's hand brushed Six's torso as he sprang into the air, both he and Six swinging their arms behind and hurling them over and in front of the net, Alan's armpits clearing the top just a hair faster than Six. The kid had lift. More importantly, it was a coordinated block.

How'd that feel?

Good, like, um, yeah, I didn't have to think about it as much.

Right! And you shouldn't. Clearly, you've done well without it. Even without me calling it out, just think about having your antenna aware of both the other team and ours. But you don't have to actually look that hard for it.

Thanks, Six!

No problem.

When they thumped each other's shoulder blades, Six gave a few light taps to Alan's low back and Alan squeezed Six's shoulder. They hadn't scrimmaged on the same side much, so this two-person huddle felt both unfamiliar and more intimate. In teaching him the Six-th sense, she was reminding herself it was hers.

Pete blew a whistle and the moment was gone. Sam had just entered and looked bleary, as if it hadn't been a full forty-five minutes since he'd gotten off the bus. He glanced at Alan and Six hugging and met Six's eyes. She lifted her chin his way and began to jog alongside Alan.

###

Regalado's first team lift of the tournament was a jet-lagged and grouchy go. The usually peppy Ricky barely nodded at Green when they saw each other boarding the bus. Sonus managed to clear another gym and move up Regalado's schedule so they no longer had the morning off. Green was warming up alone in the hotel fitness center when she found out.

The arena weight room smelled like no one had ever sweat in it before them. As Griffin did his squats without weights,

Green wondered if he had been moved to learn more about the victims from scrolling through his phone's newsfeed that morning. But none of the boys seemed to know or care. What did it have to do with them? Grief for strangers could only coalesce in public a couple times a year and people from marginalized backgrounds were murdered all the time.

If no one was talking about it, Green certainly wouldn't bring it up. She racked 20 kg on either side of the bar and rubbed the slick, ropey tissue above her knees. Just another lift. Griffin was nowhere near a weight of any kind. He held one foot up to his butt for a quad stretch, resting his other hand on the wall for support, not even trying to engage his core. Green wondered how much the nepo baby was getting paid to be a completely useless libero, typically the lowest-paid position because, like so many ball sports, volleyball valued brute-force offense more than skilled defense.

Griffin's reserve Will was doing jumping squats with ankle weights and a small dumbbell in each hand. This kid was so ready, so good, and would probably only play ten minutes this whole tournament. While Griffin stretched his other quad, Will strapped a tire on a chain to a thick belt around his waist and ploughed across the length of the gym, ankle weights and all.

Hey!

Green turned to see Walt setting up at the squat rack next to hers. Hey, Walt. How's it goin'?

I'm good. You?

Green blew a wispy out of her face, only for it to flop right back down. She rolled her eyes and in one motion undid her ponytail and shook out her thick black hair. As it glistened in the harsh LED lighting, she noticed Walt eyeing her with disgust. Or was that envy?

As Green re-did her ponytail, Walt wondered whether she just had more hair follicles on her scalp than her.

Green still hadn't given a verbal response. Sorry, I'm okay. Rough night.

Right? I'm exhausted. Walt did a set of warm-up squats with just the barbell.

Right. I'm glad they found us this gym.

Same, same.

Walt was the only other Asian person on Regalado, besides one of the assistant coaches. But as Green had written in her post last night, Asian America was not a monolithic community and often she had no idea how to talk to him. She wasn't sure how much of her reticence came from Walt being the other setter. What was she supposed to say to him: Sorry, you probably won't get to play unless I retire or you transfer?

It's nice to put my body back together before actual practice, Green tried, not quite believing her own delivery. Guthrie would be disappointed.

Totally, Walt replied in between hip openers and knee pulses. She was getting ready to add a couple of plates to the bar. Green's post about the murders had topped her feed this morning: "As an Asian American trans woman, tonight's news pains me more than I can express in words." Should she have shown she understood? Walt's own phone was off last night. As soon as she got to her room, she did her skincare routine and passed out. She had adopted her regimen from Green's

"Go to Bed with Me" video with *The Snip*. Not that she would ever tell Green that. Before, she'd inexpertly sampled thirty products in a month and had the worst breakout of her adult life. Now, her face didn't gleam like Green's but her acne scars had mostly faded. In any case, she hadn't seen the news till a couple hours ago. Maybe Green would think it smarmy if Walt tried to express sympathy. She watched Green add an 18″ block in front her rack. Green probably wasn't in the mood to talk about something so gruesome.

Indeed, Green did not have the energy to recount the news to Walt if he himself was not going to communicate being aware of it. He may be Asian but being a man still put him in his own bubble. Maybe he had awkward faggot energy, but he was still very much a boy, very repressed in all the ways that bored her. And so, they squatted together in silence.

After each squat, Green re-racked the barbell, jumped up to the block, turned around, and pistol-squatted back down. Walt made a note to try the exercise next time Green wasn't around. Green had no business lifting all that weight while staying so thin. She had read on her forum countless reminders that girls could be muscular too, but she didn't want to be that kind of girl. If Walt matched what Green was squatting, she'd probably gain 10 lbs. on accident. Walt needed to work on her agility more than her strength. She needed more playing time.

As Green stretched a cable above her head, she tried to maintain the sensation of strength pulling up from the ground, up her calves, into her thighs, sacrum, back, and shoulders in one fluid motion. She concentrated on this momentum and not the unsettling reminder that her job paid her to take care of her body, while the world had failed those three women. She turned off her phone notifications at the gym but couldn't help wonder what might be happening. When she had written her quick post last night, she had just wanted to acknowledge the news so her followers would know that she knew. Overnight, Yemma had sent her a voice message, her voice gravelly and somber, applauding the clarity and courage in Green's post. But from the barrage of comments she'd scrolled through this morning, she was worried that she was getting attention for the wrong reason. People told her they were scared and that, like Yemma, they thought Green was brave. Brave for what?

###

Green you really do it all. A professional athlete and a true activist. I'm so inspired. #protecttranslives #endasianmurders

You know what this means. You and your gook girlfriend are next!

Imagine getting patted down every time you wanna fly because your junk sets off security . . . My dysphoria could not

Green, authenticity is dangerous and expensive, don't do it!!

It's okay if you're scared to go on hormones. Just say you're a coward and leave being trans to the real girls.

How do people have time to post comments all day? Don't you people have jobs?

Weren't they putting themselves at risk by being out so late?

yeah, i got clocked for the first time in a month, idk how six and green handle this every day

Thank god Green is trans because if she was cis, she'd find a way to make this about how her parents wanted her to be a doctor and the kids said her lunch smelled

@spikycity damn I should've applied for a job at the airport, maybe I could've waved my wand along Six's inseam, maybe take her to a private room for questioning

You know, I feel like growing up Asian prepared Six and Green to navigate being outsiders on their teams

Womanhood makes woman not TERF biology @transaretrans

Why hasn't @sixsosweet said anything about this?

Green, y'all aren't practicing are you?! No way they're not canceling the tournament

No way, he's too famous to actually be killed. When's the last time someone got away with murdering anyone in his income bracket?

###

By commenting on the murders, Green had broken her pattern. Maybe it shouldn't come back. Maybe she should keep talking about this. Just a year ago, she had filled her feed with posts about politics. And then Yemma had gently suggested she might attract more sponsors with more neutral content, so she returned to posting about herself. But maybe she could have it both ways. In this horrid aftermath, now more than ever, the intentional development of her content could make a true difference for her community. It was her responsibility to do everything within her sphere of influence to make sure this would never happen again. Surely there'd be brands who would want to support her message. As she dreamed about a safe future for Asian trans women and all QTBIPOC communities, Green felt the energy whir through her fingertips. She was built for this.

As she moved to the stationary bikes, Green thought about her fight with Six after their Live two weeks ago. Maybe they should have deviated from the score. Why was Green able to modify her personal content calendar to acknowledge last night's horrific events but *Six & Green* wasn't? Green set the resistance just to increase blood flow before actual practice. Sometimes when you went off-script, the spontaneity could attract new audiences and more sustained attention. But if it was a disaster, it'd compromise the integrity of the entire brand. They'd have to talk about the murders this week, she decided. She began mentally preparing to converse naturally with her partner of nearly two years. With her breezy affability, Six would welcome this change of heart without fuss. Green realized she hadn't even texted Six that she was at the arena four hours earlier than planned. For all the time she put into social media, she could be a little forgetful about communicating.

Walt joined her on the bikes and programmed an interval set. Was he trying to intimidate her? Green wondered if Walt's friends had had to get used to him. If he even had any.

As Walt began pedaling, she wondered if Green had ever considered an athleisure sponsorship. Walt could picture her running with cool magnanimity in a bright lilac set. Walt knew she could never do it but liked knowing Green could.

Green watched her legs pumping beneath her and felt that she was training for something bigger. Her 753k followers (as of this morning) would buy anything to support her. She was training for Sonus but maybe a new chapter of trans life too. They would end transmisogyny in all forms, from murderous hate crime to bigoted thinking. And if she made it to 1 million followers with her abilities, maybe Lulumelon would get back to Yemma. She knew they weren't ignoring her because of the shape of her legs. But still, Green pedaled faster.

All right, that's time! Oliver called.

He stood close to the bikes so while everyone gathered around, Walt kept pedaling. A droplet streamed down her face. How was Green not sweating?

So, how's everyone feeling? Oliver hadn't said a word on the bus that morning, but maybe he would now. Sweat off some of that jet lag? Well, you have an hour for lunch. There's food by the picnic tables outside where you can break, otherwise, stay safe, and meet you at the main court.

The team began clearing out. Green looked at them, at Walt still pedaling, at all these men. Really? That was it?

###

Outside the weight room, team Aracaju waited to enter the gym in their marigold tracksuits. Her mask back on, Green looked for her friends Henry (6′0″, 165 lbs., #28), Aracaju's star outside with the fastest serve but the goofiest face, and Curtis (6′5″, 197 lbs., #3), a middle with the broadest block.

Girls! Green squealed.

Curtis shouted, Let's Go! and Henry squealed back. Green and Six were the only girl girls in the league, or at least the only out ones. The three of them collided in a group hug, Green's forehead knocking Henry's chin and her ponytail flipping against Curtis's hair. Both boys gave her the Aracaju double-butt tap and she returned the favor. With them, butts were just butts. With them, she could embody that louder version of herself that felt cramped with Regalado. They were all Americans—Curtis Black and Henry Chinese—who thought they'd retire after NCAL only to play pro ball abroad. Six and Green had managed to coordinate a trip to visit them in Brazil last fall. Even though they weren't the kind of friends that kept in touch week to week, they had seen each other sweat and get frustrated and excited from across the net for years. Plus they were all gay.

I am *so* happy to see you both, Green said, holding each of them by the shoulder.

Girl, you look so gorgeous, does jet lag have you blocked? Curtis said.

Oh stop, Green said. Curtis, when did you dye your hair? And Henry, did you get taller?

Don't make fun of me, glamazon, Henry (6′0″) said.

As they caught up—Curtis had posted a salon selfie yesterday, how had she missed it?—she could see two of the other Aracaju boys eyeing her. They wished they were famous. Curtis's

BTS and workout vlogs had given him both a rare injury-free career and the first and only volleyball athlete sponsorship by Blue Ox, but even Green didn't care about that just now. She had to know where Curtis's winter boyfriend had gone.

Yeah, I dumped him, Curtis laughed. I don't think he understood that the season doesn't just end when he wants me to spend more time with him because his job is depressing or whatever.

What does he do again? Green asked.

He's some consultant but I never knew what for.

That is depressing. What about you, Henry? How's Piper?

I miss him so much already! Wanna see a picture?

Before Green could affirm, Henry's phone was already beneath her face, playing a video of a golden corgi trotting by the beach.

As long as they're shampooing the sand out of his fur, I'm happy!

Have you seen Six? Curtis asked.

Yes! Really quickly last night.

Wait. Henry reached for Green's elbow, his face serious. Did you see the news? About the . . . are you okay?

Oh wow, yes. I did. It's . . .

I saw your post, Curtis said. How are you feeling?

I don't know? It was nice to work out honestly—

Oh my god! There she is!

Czwartek, fresh from stadium practice, headed their way, and most important among them was Six and her glorious hair making her the easiest hot girl to spot from a mile away.

Green! Six called. Oh my god, Curtis, Henry! Six squeezed between Sam and Pete and ran over.

They'd been in the same city for nearly a day and had barely seen each other, so when Six grabbed Green and hugged her tight, she almost started crying again. A loop of her mask slipped off one of her ears but Green's cheek pressed it to her face. Green turned to Henry and Curtis, who had a delicate hand at his throat, his eyes shining. Girls! Six exclaimed. How are you?!

We're good!

Henry! Curtis! their coach called. I know you're excited to fangirl your rivals but if you're not squeezing a barbell in two minutes . . .

Got it, Luke! they responded together. Even their coach had to acknowledge Six and Green's power.

We were just talking about those awful murders from yesterday, Curtis said. I'm sure you heard?

Ugh, yeah. Green and I were crying about it last night.

I'm so sorry. Henry patted their shoulders.

Thanks, Six said. I don't even—

Did your team mention it at all in practice? asked Green.

You mean like the coaches?

Or just like, anyone? said Green.

Uhh. Six tried to recall. No, no one said anything.

Really! Henry said. That's so surprising.

Is it? Six asked. You mean would a bunch of bros who just got off a plane and want to win a big sports tournament want to remember that one of their teammates—

I see your point, Henry said. But they should say something!

Cis allies always wanted cis people to do better. Curtis nodded, vigorously.

I guess I just expect so little from them, Six said. Obviously it's incredible playing with Czwartek. But as far as I know they're literally all straight. And I feel like people are tired of the news.

Yep, they definitely moved on from last year, Curtis said.

Curtis! Henry! Lift! Luke called from the doorway.

Coming!

Well, at least we're all together now, Henry said. You gonna be okay?

Green shifted to her right hip. It's definitely weird, but yeah, I'll be fine. Don't worry about us.

We won't! Henry said. We're just preparing to crush you both. See you later.

Curtis nodded, his expression flat but his hugs to Green and Six full and warm. We'll see you tonight at the hotel?

From seven feet apart in the hotel courtyard! Six called as they walked away. Lift good, girls! To Green, she asked, Are you guys on lunch too?

Now we are.

Wow, shout out to Sonus changing your schedule for you and me. Let's go?

Please! Green threaded her fingers in Six's.

Do you think they'll say anything at practice? You know, maybe folks will check the news or something during the break or, I don't know.

Maybe.

Honestly, I'm kind of glad no one tried to ask me to pardon their contrived guilt or whatever.

Wait, how did practice go?

Six had felt miserable just hours ago but that moment with Alan made her feel like she had agency in her small life. She looked around conspiratorially before leaning over in a stage whisper, Sam was—

Green! Six! Our stars! A plain-faced white man of average height emerged from some nowhere door.

Phil! Six said, her arms open with generosity. It's so nice to see you in person.

Beneath her mask, Green stretched her cheek muscles. Hi, Phil.

The Sonus VP reached for the two Asian American women with seasoned possessiveness. Even though it was an obvious business move, Phil had been the one to suggest sponsoring Six and Green as star players this season. You're both set for your shoot tomorrow? We just sent your agents the final script.

We can't wait, Six said.

Good, good! We're so excited to watch you play on our new network. And with live audiences!

After five years of using ESTN to grow its viewership, Sonus was ready to ditch Daddy and launch their own streaming service.

Thanks, Green said, nodding gravely. She'd heard subscriber conversion had been modest during the regular season soft launch, so knew tomorrow's shoot was critical to them all. Still, if they we're going to continue doing business, she'd have to ask Guthrie to help finesse these conversations.

Is there anything either of you need? Hotel and facilities are okay? Czwartek was in the arena this morning, right? Isn't it just gorgeous, Six?

It's incredible, she said, her enthusiastic nod convincing.

Six was so good at dealing with strange men. Green could handle Curtis and Henry, or her team. But watching Phil pat Six's bicep like a bro made her feel ill. At least he would never try that with tiny girl Green.

Well, our break is only so long, Green began.

Right, of course! I'll let you . . . ladies get to it! Phil winked.

Once outside, Green breathed in the fresh air, a bit thinner with the elevation but much more crisp than she was used to back home. Players from Czwartek, Regalado, and two insignificant teams sat at separate picnic tables.

Ugh, I forgot about that, Six said, surveying the boy-yard, the full bloom of spring trees. He couldn't just ask to touch my bicep?

I know, Green said, I'm thankful for the sponsorship and their investment in the sport and all but . . . She sighed. Privately, she was actually excited to show off some moves in a more plainly promotional way than Regalado's standard realist shots. At least Phil gave them the chance to get filmed from all angles tomorrow. To appeal to Six, Green said, At least we won't be the only ones?

True. It does make us look less like the special edition trans girls, you know?

Hate to break it to you, but I think we're always gonna be the special edition trans girls.

Ugh, you're right, baby. Six turned to see bros from all corners of the courtyard waving her over.

Do you wanna hang out with everyone or be antisocial?

Honestly, I want to be antisocial. We won't really be allowed later, right?

True, Green said.

Let's say a quick hi but run off?

Green tried to move with as much conviction as Six so it didn't look like she was just following her girlfriend around. Green watched as people said hi to them both but held Six's gaze longer or extended an arm to fist-bump her first. Was it because Green came off less friendly? Maybe it was because Six managed to distinguish Anthony from Anton from Antony without hesitating. Maybe Green was just a bitch. And/or maybe they kept their distance and made themselves less memorable because Green couldn't bro like her girlfriend could bro . . . Green had circled these questions too many times. If only her confirmation bias worked on remembering boys' names.

At least Six could be counted on to make quick work of this. They escaped the manfield in mere minutes. Soggy wraps in one hand, they both took off their masks and paused. Six reached over to touch Green's fleshy cheek, the line of her jaw. I wish I could kiss you, she said. Even though the COVIS protocol seemed fake during meals, being the lone it girls only made the rules realer for them. Maybe if the bros kissed each other first, COVIS would disappear forever.

Green asked again, So how did practice go? Did you take your spot?!

Six leaned in as if they weren't already out of earshot of any person. When parents lectured about being a good sport, they always meant not being a sore loser or gloating to the other team. Hardly anyone talked about how to handle wiping the floor with someone on your own team. You had to consider people's feelings when you sweat with them every day and hoped they wouldn't spike a ball at your nose on "accident." Six and Green had understood this acutely since they'd first come out.

Well, Six chewed, Sam shows up late and he's just sluggish. He barely trots when we're jogging, he keeps dropping the ball when we're just doing ball control, he rolls out when we're planking. Pete was giving him the "You're a professional, you know your own body, we just got off a long flight," blah blah blah.

He did look kinda subdued when we just passed him. Green made to turn around but Six grabbed her knee. Wait, it's too soon.

Sorry, I'm curious! Green said.

Six waved in the direction of a player who must have seen Green looking over and continued in a lower voice, So when we start playing, Pete starts messing with some of the starting combos, but just the hitters and libero.

Uh-huh.

And Sam is still a mess! Dan sets him the ball and he hits it into the net. And then Vinny sets me the ball and I spike it in between his arms.

Does Pete say anything?

Not directly. We break to wipe the court and after, he puts me with the starters and Sam is opposite me.

What?! Green slapped the air just above the table. Has he ever done this?

Like during regular season home practice. But never at a travel game or before a tournament.

So did he make anything official?

Nope, I mean, it's only the first day we're here. I feel like Sam probably has some time. But seeds were planted!

Wait, how did you play when you were on the A team?

I was amazing! Just having Alan know about the Six-th sense helped us be in such better sync. And with the two of us breathing together, the other five sank into it too. I haven't felt the starting team move like that all season. In one play, Vinny tried to do a dump but I saw it and called it out and James re-positioned just in time and Alan, sweet boy, he got the block out! Which he's done before but it looked so definitive today!

Green set her fork down and remembered her phone, which she still hadn't checked since the morning. A whoosh of air swirled in her stomach. Six! Green said, returning to the moment. That's so amazing. That quickly?!

I know! Like I really felt it there just now, you know? The Six-th sense, she whispered. She laughed, her hair dancing effortlessly. I hope we get to build on it this afternoon.

I know, babe, I hope so. Green let loose her own hair and willed it to catch a little breeze but it just slunk at her back.

What if we joked about it on our next show?

Joked about what, little lady?

My Six-th sense! We could ask the viewers to guess which player I've worked with who doesn't have it.

And when Sam gets benched, how's that gonna age? Green's tone sounded derisive, even to her.

Six chuckled, now nervous too. She was asking to go off script again. I don't know, it was just a joke.

Oh, um. Green realized what she'd just done. Whoops. I'm sorry. I support you. Obviously. Like I want Sam to get benched, it's why I said it.

No, you're right, we don't have to make a thing of it.

Are you sure? I didn't mean—

The whole thing about being trans lesbians means we don't have to be painfully sensitive about every single little thing. I'm good if you're good.

Six hadn't meant to put herself in the position of reassuring Green when it was Green who had just dismissed her idea again. She couldn't help but refract this little flub through their little argument a couple of weeks ago. She knew it always took them a day or so to readjust to each other but this was feeling different. Even now, Green still looked guilty, so Six asked, How are you feeling now? The murders? Or that we're like, actually here?

Green paused. I don't know, honestly. I'm just so relieved to finally see you, baby.

Am I as tall as you remember?

Six! Oh my god! Seriously! She slapped her girlfriend's shoulder. Her girly roleplay wasn't original but at least she was looped in.

Green was woman enough to notice how Six had

effortlessly guided them away from a silly fight again. Green returned to the original question: I don't like feeling this disconnected from the rest of the world. Our communities are devastated right now. I'm devastated. And we're stuck in a bubble with bros who don't seem to care.

Or maybe they haven't heard yet, Six said.

Maybe. Green took a glum bite from her wrap.

Honestly? Think about who we play with. It really wouldn't surprise me if they're in the original kind of bubble too. Some people literally do not have any connection to the news.

They looked at the marketably diverse group of boys Sonus had convened in this new, globalized league. Boys with their lunches and phones, their boy jokes and boy gossip. Their teams had curated the best players from national and continental leagues, bringing everyone together in a cocktail party of extra cosmopolitan athletes. Some were publicly gay, a few more privately bicurious. A few had doping exemptions for ADHD meds, many nursed secret injuries they hoped could wait out the tournament. Nearly all the starters posted action shots captured by their team photographers on a weekly basis, if not more frequently, and revealed their off-court alliances in likes and comments on each other's posts. Bro, I'm still mad about that point but with a perfect swing like that, you deserved it. This public record of parasocializing showed that to most of them, Six and Green were indifferent acquaintances, mutual follows for show. Green had already counted how many of her colleagues followed Six but not Green. Combining user behavior data with player data, the boy league's resident ladies could guess who privately thought them girl-freak attention whores sucking up all the sponsorship money. At least they'd never whine "biological advantages."

It's just weird how after all these years, these people still don't know how to talk to us. Green didn't like her distant bro colleagues' posts either, didn't try to break the ice post-game. But for her, it came to the same point. The cis boys weren't marginalized for being cis boys, so they should extend the hand.

Well, I mean, these people talk to us. Or me, at least. But they talk to us about what they know. It's generic small talk you make with colleagues you only see a few times a year. Hey, how's the season going? Or, cool shoes, bro! Like, they're still scared of offending us. They're not going to come up to us and say, *Sorry for your loss,* or, *We care about trans people.*

I'd rather that than this complete nonacknowledgment.

Right, but besides your post, we haven't brought it up with them either.

But why should we have to talk about it first?

It would be impossible to say which came first—the girls being aloof and intimidating to protect themselves or volley-bro culture making them feel like they had to.

I know, babe. The volleyball community isn't a community in the same way that the Asian community or the trans community or the Asian trans girl community are things. And, those are barely even things.

Barely even things, Six echoed. Uh-oh.

Green turned back to face the crowd. A boy was walking over.

Do you know him? Green asked.

We might've played him but I do not recognize his face—hi!

Six, oh my god! Hi!

Kevin was such a big fan. His team had played against Six earlier that season, before he was starting. He asked to take a selfie, with Green in it too, as an afterthought. Kevin crossed to their side of the table and squeezed between them. When Six took his phone, Green could see Kevin's youthful face glowing in her periphery and between her girlfriend's hands. It was his first season in the league.

Thanks so much, you guys—I mean, girls—I mean, ladies.

Correct! Six winked.

Of course. It's so nice to meet you, Kevin, Green said.

It was like yesterday at the airport, except Green had to see her girlfriend being more popular than her in the flesh and not just through a screen.

What a cutie! Six said, her head tilted to one side. Should we go inside?

Green slung her duffel over one shoulder and grabbed both of their trash.

Six went on, What were we saying? Oh yeah, community isn't real.

We are not in this together.

Nope, Six said, eyeing her phone. And he definitely follows you but didn't talk to you.

Nope!

Let's talk about it more tonight? Six said. Maybe we can ask the league to do something or make a statement. Maybe they already have. Tournaments always feel like these weird bubbles. But we can speak outside of it too if you think that would help?

Green felt her shoulders drop. You always reassure me so much, Six. I love you.

Aww, of course. I love you, Green! Discipline was eating right and not kissing your girlfriend during a pandemic.

It's funny how before we got here, you were anxious and I wasn't, and now that we're here, I'm kinda anxious and you're so calm.

It just doesn't feel like there's much else we can do. We have a job and the job is to beat each other.

You mean, your job is to start so that you can lose to me properly.

Green! Six slapped at Green's hip and pulled her close.

Green still hadn't checked her phone. She didn't want to see the notifications on her screen unless she actually had the attention span to deal with them. Instead, here they were, holding each other and saying things they had said before, both of them kind of acknowledging the murders but also pretending as if they weren't already exhausted, and the day was barely half over.

###

Green are you okay?? You didn't get that fake virus did you?

I feel like Green barely acknowledged that they were sex workers. Pretty disappointed that she's whorephobic :(

Did Six make it to the tournament?! I'm so worried about her

Which embarrassing famous women do we think Green modeled herself after? So I can choose someone else?

Maybe if we had universal health care, we could stab Green with some estrogen

Did it occur to your racist mind so used to loud Americans that maybe Green's more stoic because of her Japanese upbringing?

Six probably got COVIS

I know it can get really toxic in here but these places have taught me everything I know about how to treat trans people

I don't think any of you could understand how traumatic being an Asian trans woman public figure expected to be vulnerable and relatable at all times is

Green, we're gonna KILL this man. The murderer's my boyfriend's cousin, like do you think we should call the cops?

Are you kidding? Green paid for her orchi out of pocket

If any trans people are scared in Alpharetta and need a cis-shield or a safe place, DM me anytime

You don't think we can tell that pic of you crying is from three weeks ago?! You're not only fake, you're insulting our intelligence

Maybe Green just has resting bitch face

Yeah, and then I heard her coaches made her sew her balls back on because she wasn't hitting hard enough

Green are you gonna be at the virtual vigil with @sexworkiswork ??

Green, are you still playing in the tournament after what's happened? I feel like Six would obvi, but you're actually a part of our community and you care about us!

@everyourgreen why didn't you say their names. Suzy Akhter! Clarisse Valdez! Bea Tran! #protecttranslives #endasianmurders

Any relationship Six and Green have to our community is shallow and opportunistic, if you buy into their charade, that's your fault!

Wait, I thought that excuse conveniently leaked because her doc got nervous and botched it

###

He (@transaretrans, 82k followers) had had enough of Green. He didn't find her insufferable because she was trans—he definitely wasn't transphobic. Trans women are women! He'd say it if anyone asked. But if Six and Green were so committed to being women, they should go through the work of being women. They should play for the women's league! They'd have to deal with more transphobic nonsense than they already did, but sports couldn't be fair unless everyone was equalized, including Six and Green's Y chromosomes.

He was impatient with Green because he wanted more for her. Instead of realizing the potential of her divine transfeminine power, Green relied on special treatment from Regalado and the entire league for being a special fucking fairy unicorn when, biologically, she was still just a boy with long hair who apparently had no interest in making her womanhood biological. Green got to partake in male privilege and social justice warrior trans privilege at the same time. At least her also conveniently hot trans girlfriend Six had taken a hit to her standing this season.

Six had been much less annoying to him than Green lately. She didn't try so hard. It was almost like she knew the little gender gimmick was a ruse to make up for her average skill and talent. He almost admired her for making the grift work. But Green seemed to really believe what she said all the time. She acted personally heartbroken at the murders, as if she knew the victims, and personally frightened, as if she could ever be at risk of that kind of violence. A textbook and unsubtle narcissist, making everything about her.

And now Six and Green were together again, walking down the hallways of the arena cosplaying the popular couple in high school, giggling like there weren't murders to be sad about. They were *so* jejune. He hadn't dated anyone since the pandemic, because he'd been busy being an adult. At dinner earlier, they held court in the courtyard and people kept asking them for selfies. Enabling them! By deferring to Six and Green's supremacy, these groveling fanboys were undercutting their own bottom line. He was a staunch anti-capitalist *and* people being *so* bad at business got him *so* mad. If you were gonna play the game, play it well. Win! Growing up, his family could've been lower-middle class but instead, he grew up pathetic poor because his dad kept lending money they barely had so his hapless friends could start the worst businesses. So these boys posting their novelty selfies with the poster girls to try to siphon little droplets off of their clout was fundamentally triggering.

Six and Green already made more money, they already had more clout, which would only make them more money in the future. If Six and Green were gonna make a profitable spectacle of their gender, so would he. He was not like his dad. He would be good at business.

His purpose became clear after their maudlin make-out media circus from last year's tournament. Seeing them capitalize on the world's devastating isolation with their manipulative dramatics inspired a political awakening. He began to reevaluate everything he thought he understood about gender and biology and social constructs. By trying so desperately to convince the world what pretty girls they were without transitioning, Six and Green were making fundamental trans needs seem superfluous in a time when trans rights were already under attack. Green's overcompensations weren't just embarrassing. They endangered the livelihoods of trans people in actual need. He couldn't confront this without getting dismissed himself, so he decided to create an anonymous account. He was stepping up to protect trans people.

To convey his message, he had to broaden his scope beyond Six and Green. They were famous enough to justify recurring guest appearances, but he recognized that volleyball was an insular community. He had to offer his audience an equal-opportunity transgender-critical analysis. He told nuanced stories of trans men playing women's rugby, of butch trans women wearing blazers, of young adult they/thems microdosing. He was rigorous in his research. He once thought this pro lifter was trans but alas, he just looked like that.

Lounging in his hotel armchair after a long day, @transaretrans opened his phone's folder full of trans people screenshots and anecdotes. He chose a screenshot of Six taking a dance class with some ballerina. It was such a Green-tinged move. Poor guileless Six. He rolled his eyes and made fists with his man hands. He breathed deeply, trying to slow the flow of air in and out of his prodigious lungs like his therapist had taught him. Trust in your plan, he told himself. He relaxed his hands and opened his eyes.

Over the last year, he had developed a buzzwordy style that algorithmized his followers' attention spans and kept them coming back. He began typing:

> Our eyes on the ground at the upcoming Sonus Volleyball Tournament have heard some troubling rumors. If the developments we've heard today pan out, then you'll know exactly what we're talking about. #transaretrans

He posted. Everyone had secret lives and incomprehensible incoherences they dumped online but hid from people who would find them unforgiveable. His therapist didn't need to know about @transaretrans. This wasn't who he was. It was just something he had to do.

He returned to @transaretrans and scanned the initial trickle of likes and comments. One day, it'd be in the thousands before his phone could even refresh. Green's ambitious team would make a futile attempt to have the page taken down for defamation or bullying but he knew Instagraph would take his side.

He checked his personal account, where he'd shared a photo with Green to his story earlier today. He didn't like it, but he couldn't not play along. And she hadn't even viewed it yet. Even if the rumor he'd heard about high follower accounts being given the option to hide read receipts was true, this was just another sign of how arrogant she had become. He could've been any man obsessing over them through a liquid crystal display. But @transaretrans would have the fleshy memories of VIP access to Six and Green for the duration of the tournament. He knew what they'd smelled like today and no amount of Green's knockoff designer perfume could mask the rank stench of her desperate sweat. He turned off his phone and plotted how he could put Six and Green in their place without interrupting their profit potential. More than anyone would care to admit, his future, like that of every man in the league, depended on these two very beautiful women.

###

The next morning, Six awoke to staccato buzzes from her phone. It was Green sharing more exciting updates. She didn't even have to look. She yawned, blinking till the small morning tears slid onto her pillow. These weren't grief tears. Her eyes were always wet when she woke. Her vision sharpened and the world she was reentering slowly took shape: the tournament, the murders, this bubble of indifferent boys that enveloped them. After a petite sigh, she SpaceTimed her girlfriend.

Omg, Six, it hasn't stopped! Green's phone faced the bathroom mirror image of her patting goop into her face.

Morning, dear, Six replied, her voice bleary.

Morning! All these activists and influencers are messaging me and they want to like, vid chat when we're off practice tonight and the Sex Work Is Work Collective wants me to be a panelist in a conversation about the murders for some reason, and I just can't believe this is happening and wait did you just wake up, we have the shoot later, did you go over the scripts and pack your makeup bag last night?

Six sat up. Maybe she should've sat with her dread a minute longer before calling her girlfriend. How are you feeling about it all?

Overwhelmed! Green said before Six had finished asking the question. She rolled her eyes but she was also smiling faintly. It was soothing to feel like she had a connection to this grief that took her out of her own heart. She wasn't just sad. She had a reinvigorated sense of purpose in this world. Being a face people attached to the most recent episode of mass murder could feel like a burden. But Green was trying to see it as an opportunity. A responsibility. With so many people now predisposed to sympathize with her, she could make them listen. She could do it all. She looked at her sleepy girlfriend and wondered if this might enliven Six's attitude toward social media. I'm so thankful. I obviously wasn't trying to get this kind of attention with that post.

Right, Six said, once again horizontal in bed. When she'd suggested asking Sonus to make a statement, she was thinking about it hypothetically, as if two other Asian trans pro athletes would pick up the baton. In reality, Brett and Yemma had worked overnight to prepare a script and now they had to get it produced. Six wouldn't have even made her own public statement if she could have avoided it. But better to say anything canned than not acknowledge it at all. Last night, she captioned a selfie of her masked face smooshed against a bus window with a short paragraph saying she'd made it to the tournament safe and healthy (so far) and was absolutely devastated by the news but didn't have much to add to the topic just yet. She would take her time to process the event between practices and matches but advised her fans not to expect much from her till after the tournament.

But like, Green went on, it's also so nice to feel connected with our communities while we're in this little volleyball bubble. Thank god for the internet! Wait, did you prep for today?

Six rolled to her other side, leaving her phone facing the ceiling. I mean, I looked it over. It wasn't that much text. And don't worry, I won't forget my face again.

Sixy! Ugh, I wish I had it as easy as you.

Six told herself that Green was obviously talking about today's upcoming film shoot, not the shooting of their sisters or Six's entire existence. She rubbed the skin beneath her ribs. Gweenie. You're great at this! Are you going to do that panel?

I asked Yemma about it and she's in contact with them.

Not about money!

No! Of course not. About recording and archiving and editing. Are you feeling ready for today?

It seemed Green would keep asking the question. At the end of Czwartek's afternoon practice yesterday, Pete had pulled Six aside. You're looking good, he'd said. Just stay on point. Six returned the assurance in his gaze with the cool ease of a mature player who didn't need it said aloud yet. And while vanquishing an untalented man had cost her more effort than it should've, having to tap tap the pixels on her phone to transmit a compact version of her grief had depleted her. Six wasn't sure why she didn't just tell Green she was still so sad. She wished she could've called a friend who wasn't in volleyball and wasn't her girlfriend, someone who wasn't even trans or Asian. Six loved Green but talking about these murders with someone who shared all four of those things with her felt both unbearable and pointless. And only Green was in her time zone and she was processing it so differently.

Six rolled her ankles in circles and waited to feel the circulation in the arches of her feet. Her right calf refusing to lengthen was a harsh reminder of her age. Thinking about their scheme for today only intensified the lethargy in her legs. And she was jet-lagged. Okay, I'm up!

We can do this! We have to do this. It's awful, but it's our time.

The sense of purpose Green was channeling through her grief seemed unflappable, whereas Six's desire to start had already lost its potency now that it seemed possible.

Oh! Green said. She put down a brow pencil and picked up

her phone, which still showed Six's hotel room ceiling. Yemma and Brent wanna know how we feel about talking about the murders on our show this week too.

Huh. Six slid briefs up her legs. So like, sort of get into it live? What do you think?

I think we should. I think it's important to talk about it.

It is, Six agreed. Not two weeks ago, she had wanted to bring the real world into their show and Green balked. Now, Green was all for it. Six was grateful Green was asking, but now, she wasn't sure she actually wanted to comment on current events for all their fans to take too seriously. She could sound bratty over a little couple's spat but not disorganized when declaiming on systemic violence.

Great, I'll check in with Guthrie, Green said. Wait, is that a faucet? Are you up?

Yep! Six dried her hands and propped her phone against the bathroom mirror to face her directly. It fell over. Only Green could station her own phone without having to troubleshoot geometry. After Six repositioned it, what little skepticism her face betrayed was obscured by the camera angled at her waist.

Wow, okay. Hi, sexy. Did you put on underwear just for me?

Six laughed easily as she massaged moisturizer into her bare clavicle and stiff neck. Yes, babe, could never let a day pass where you forget what I look like. But also, I'm not trying to distract you too much.

Ugh, you're so thoughtful. Green blew a kiss.

Even if the impetus had changed, sustaining the rhythms of daily life had to be better than immobilizing depression.

As Green began drawing in her wing with a dark emerald-green liner, they speculated whether or not Sam would play any better today. Green politely didn't share that she'd gained 44k followers (now 797k overall) overnight and was now only 105k shy of Six, whom she'd noticed hadn't received as big of an uptick on her post as Green had. She was getting closer! She knew 44k accounts, bots included, would not actually make her more worthy a person, but she still wanted to share her excitement. Her eyes were fiercely perfect. If she finally caught up to Six, she might text her about it and say *haha*.

###

That afternoon, Six (@sixsosweet, 904k followers, Green (@everyourgreen, 801k followers), Curtis (@curtis, 439k followers), and Henry (@henryhits, 278k followers) reunited in the main arena. Sonus had assembled an entire apparatus of equipment and crew to produce three minutes of promotional content to run during the tournament. As Green felt the weight of the arena's full lights on her skin, she wondered if she'd look washed out here too.

So it looks like today's females and faggots day in men's volleyball, Henry said.

Curtis slapped Henry's arm, his eyebrows raised in faux shock. Henry! You mean girls and gays day!

Sonus had invited these four to appeal to the girls, the

gays, and the secret gays. Later, they were bringing the boy boys to film spots for the girls, gays, and the boys who were just bro-ing out over that smooth form.

As they took in the set, a light-footed man with thick forearms approached them with Phil at his side. Nick, the director of the shoot, talked them through the setup without making eye contact. Next to Nick's nonchalance, Phil's pompous *mhms* seemed particularly cartoonish. Green held her back straight as she looked at Nick but saw Phil eyeing her. Any questions? Henry! It's Henry, right?

Henry nodded breezily. His fifteen seconds of fame would be constructed first.

Don't fuck it up, Curtis shouted.

Bro! Henry mocked.

What? We believe in you!

Six egged him on further. We believe that you won't put us behind schedule.

Thanks for all the support, guys! Henry rolled his eyes and began warming up.

Wow, that's just lovely, Phil remarked with a pat on Six's shoulder. What beautiful camaraderie! And you don't even play on the same team.

That depends on what team you're considering, Curtis said.

Green smirked, her contribution to the conversation hidden behind her face mask.

Well, I'm just so excited for you all to help promote Sonus Sports' new streamer, Phil said. I'm sure you'll bring in so many new subscribers.

A PA pulled Curtis to block his shoot, leaving Six and Green alone with Phil. His roving eyes were even more unabashed than yesterday. This should make their plan easier to pull off.

I just hope I'll get to play more this tournament! Six began.

Phil nodded with grave sympathy. We're just going to have to get you starting so the world can finally watch volleyball's favorite couple play each other again.

We'll see! Coach Pete hasn't set the lineup yet and you know, it might change as the tournament goes on.

Of course, of course. I just hope to see it myself. Phil winked. That clip from the final last year, it was just so touching. You two are great for sports and incredible for television.

Green jumped in, It was just us being us, Six being her unbearably sweet self. She pulled Six in and leaned against her shoulder and saw how the cheap tenderness sustained Phil's interest. It's so nice to finally be together, especially after the news the other night, Green pressed on.

Oh. Phil placed a limp-wristed hand above his heart. Oh, of course! Absolutely, I can't even fathom what it must be like for you two right now.

It's really tough, honestly, Six said, her chin lowered but her eyes holding Phil's steady.

I'm so sorry you're having to deal with this right now. Is there anything that I or Sonus can do to support you?

Oh, that's so kind of you to ask, Phil, um, Six trailed off.

You know, Green began, it would be great if the league could release a special statement, or even a video or something, just to acknowledge the terrible incident, you know?

Express your support for Asian trans women! She knew Guthrie would've suggested a subtler approach, but she got the feeling it didn't matter, that Phil would follow her face anywhere.

Phil nodded gravely. Thanks for that idea, Green. That's fantastic! I'd have to clear it with my team first. But wait! What if you two delivered it in a video?

Us? Six said, as if the idea had never occurred to her. Wow, I mean . . .

It's perfect! You're already here, we already have the cameras set up, and I know from your show what great orators you'll be.

Aw, Phil, that's so nice. Green blinked twice.

We could just film something and I'll have my team okay it later. What do you say?

Green looked at her girlfriend, theatrically. Well, technically, we should ask our teams too, she said. Mind if we just call them real quick?

Sure, no problem. I don't think they'll be ready for your scene for a bit anyway.

We'll be right back. With their arms around each other, the beautiful couple turned around. Behind Six, Henry was walking through his path to hit a series of targets with balls that would blast from a training machine. Once in the lobby, Green made a three-way call.

Green! Brent said, his voice rich and deep on speakerphone. I hope this is the call we—

So yes, Green said, we're gonna film something, but they don't have anything prepared.

I knew you could do it! Yemma said. We'll send over our script in fifteen.

Thanks, you two, Six said. Love you for being there.

Aw, Six, Brent said. C'mon, for something as small as this? Need anything else?

Nope, we're good! See you, bro baby! Bye, Yemma! Six said.

Bye, hot girls, Brent replied.

Bye, you two! Green said.

Remember, Green, speak slowly and breathe, Yemma said, already typing away.

Brent was very much the manager for Six and Yemma the agent for Green.

Back inside, Green held the door and eased it into the frame so the heavy click wouldn't distract Henry, who was telling the camera, Our commentators? A hit! He spiked the ball through a Sonus-branded target. Our streaming platform . . . a HIT! His arm blurred around its shoulder, sending another ball into the last target. What do you have to do? Get your Sonus Sports subscription—he smacked one last ball into the bleachers—and hit it! He winked at the camera.

Green felt the flush of nervous sweat. Envy was only misdirected admiration, really. The way he varied his inflection. The way his face looked relaxed on screen. If he wasn't a natural like Six, he hid his effort much better than Green.

Cut! Nick called. That was great, Henry. I think we got it.

Ladies, you're back! Phil called.

Green shared their spontaneous update and Six solidified the stakes: It feels like such an opportune time for Sonus to align itself with the right side of history and show that, in these uncertain times, they truly support us as players in the league.

Wow, that's so brilliant. Let me email that to the team.

Can we get Six and Green set up, please? Nick called.

They rehearsed it once while Curtis filmed his spike drill in the opposite side of the arena: After a long day, you know what really—Curtis paused mid-sentence and winked—hits the spot? Curtis winks again. Volleyball.

So much winking, one had to wonder if multiple meanings were possible.

While they reviewed his second take, Green paced. She was nervous. Six squeezed her hand. They were all unmasked now, an exception for the promo of course. And with it, Six could reassure Green with the mere curve of her lips.

Alrighty, Six and Green to set!

After Curtis's moody shot, the crew blasted the lighting. Six buckled from a flash of dizziness and caught herself by the tops of her knees. She had muscled herself into the day's flow and suddenly felt out of it. Jumping from the political imperative to vindicate a hate crime to hawking subscriptions with hardly a beat between made their little scheme feel slimy. As she rubbed her kneecaps, she didn't see her body but two joints propping up her billboard face.

Six? Nick called.

Yeah! She saw knees again. No one seemed to have noticed her brief lapse. Green was floating a ball between her fingertips. For their shot, they would pass the ball back and forth, delivering their lines in between while approaching the net till finally, Green would set the ball far off into the stands and deliver the line: But the only thing that makes a game worth playing. Six would chime in: Or a game worth watching. And together: Is having your support. They would interlace their fingers through the net. This reference didn't need a wink.

They had it in two takes.

That really was splendid, Curtis said. If nothing else convinced the world what a perfect couple you two are, then . . . He tossed up his hands in resignation.

That made me wish I was in a relationship with you, you wonderful players! Phil said, now at their side from out of nowhere.

Before Six or Green had to respond, Nick emerged from video village doing neck circles as he massaged his traps. All labor passed through the body. Last shot!

While a flurry of PAs loosened the net and rolled a noisy cart of balls into a new corner, the females and faggots gathered around Nick.

Ok, so this one's pretty simple, he began. You each have your one solo line and you're gonna wait for me to give you this cue—he raised his arm and sliced it down in front of him like a guillotine. Look right into the camera, say your line. When the camera moves around and I give this cue—he raised the guillotine—run to your left to stay out of frame and just wait around this mark—Nick jogged just offset the camera—here. Once everyone's looped around, you'll all say, "Sonus Sports! Streaming the sharpest volleyball," and we're done. Any questions?

We're ready! Six said.

Let's go! Curtis said.

The door opened. It was boy boy time: Alan (6'6", 198 lbs., #4), the baby-faced outside for Czwartek; Griffin (6'3", 195 lbs., #17), the prodigal nepotism son for Regalado; plus the golden boys for the Ibaraki Jets, opposite Eric (6'8", 212 lbs., #8) and outside Thom (6'9", 239 lbs., #14). The way they strolled in together as if they'd agreed on a shared gait could make one wonder who the gay players really were.

Oh right! Nick said, We thought we'd save some time by starting them off with another version of this group shot so they'll get to see you guys demonstrate it first.

Green cocked her head to the side, shape-shifting her Live Grin with an accusatory slant that only Six recognized.

Everyone know everyone? Nick asked.

Six! Alan jogged ahead and reached for an affectionate, if brusque, hug, as if it had been a while. Six, caught off guard, returned the gesture with a few comparably macho pats on Alan's back.

Of course, you and Six play together. Nick said, pointlessly. And everyone else?

Yeah, we all go back, Thom said. Ibaraki's Thom and Eric were like Six and Green's cis white bro counterparts but teammates. Dynamic duos were essential to sustaining any sport.

Over the years, each of the indifferent handshakes Green had exchanged with Thom and Eric had given them a permanent place in the rolodex of her mind. Season by season, she flagged every upward climb in their career trajectories with mild resentment. Neither Thom nor Eric followed her or Six and, until Green's post about the murders, both had more followers than her but fewer than Six. These poster boys knew the significance of not being social media friends and this predictable power play had its intended effect on Green. Even earnest Alan already projected an innate ease with these players who knew him less than anyone else here.

Great! Nick continued. All right, let's see it. Boys, I mean, ladies and gents, balls or without balls for a run through?

Through meaningful glances, they reached consensus. This too was the Six-th sense. Curtis said, Let's do it with balls.

They took their places. Green kept her skull steady but let her eyes look up to see the shadows of the straights in the stands. Nick called, Action. It was the least challenging ball control any of them had to demonstrate today. When Henry passed the ball to Green, the ball seemed to suspend mid-air. Curtis's voice sounded rich and easy. The crew ran great big circles around Six, Green, Curtis, and Henry barely playing catch. The four of them had barely finished saying *sharpest* when Nick declared, We got it! Phil emerged from the stands clapping like he'd just accomplished something great too.

Wow, we had planned for more time than this, but y'all are pros, Nick said. Four scenes in less than an hour. It's almost as if you've been in front of a camera before.

Ha ha, Six said, playfully.

Who? Us? Curtis said. Henry and Curtis didn't have their own show but they hadn't grown their followers by being camera-shy. They couldn't just exist online like Thom and Eric did and have a platform materialize at their feet. Henry had his dog content and his meek thirst traps and Curtis had his new podcast interviewing athletes who were actually famous, not just volleyball famous. These four didn't become friends just because they were gay volleyball players. They were friends because they were gay volleyball players who were all hot and smart enough to understand how broadcasting their effortless expertise had become essential to their careers. When Sonus offered everyone one-year ambassador contracts, they all knew what the game was.

So, Nick called. Thom? Eric? Griffin? Alan?

Oh wait, just one moment! Phil checked his phone. Yes, great. Six, Green, your team sent it over. They work quickly!

Ooh, sent what? Curtis said, his voice dry for gossip.

Oh, we're just gonna film a separate package commenting on the Alpharetta murders.

That's great. So important, Henry said.

Was it? Six thought.

I know, Green said. Thanks again, Phil, for being so receptive!

Nick! Phil said. We're going to film just one more spot with Green and Six, nothing fancy. Just a quick statement we pulled together. You could film it anywhere.

And um, is there a script? Nick eyed Six and Green suspiciously.

Yes, Phil handed Nick his phone. We could just do it here.

Nick scrolled through statement. No, no, let's do it right. But I want to get the other boys in while we have the arena set up like this first. Six, Green, do you mind waiting a few?

Uh, Six paused. Czwartek was practicing soon. Alan was cleared but she didn't want to be late.

We can wait, right, Six? Green asked, her eyes shining.

Sure, Six said. Let's do it.

On the boys' first take, Griffin set the ball through one of the net's antennae. It still reached Eric but the camera caught the vibrating rod. Not a clean play they'd want to show off to the public.

Six's knees bounced as she willed the straights to get it together.

The second take, Griff sailed it way above and Eric had to jump over one of the televisions lining the court to catch it, which gave a sleek enough action shot that Nick accepted.

That'll differentiate it from ours, Green whispered.

True, Six said, tense.

All right, scene! Six and Green, let's do this! Nick called.

Phil told the director of photography how he wanted Six and Green framed and lit, as if he wouldn't have any ideas of his own, while Nick directed the camera crew to face the first row of stands.

Czwartek's afternoon practice had started three minutes ago. Pete had texted Six back, All good. Take your time. Did he mean she could take her time because she wasn't relevant anyway?

Six and Green stood in position for a test shot.

Splendid! Phil said. Shall we run it?

Just a sec! Nick said from behind the monitor.

Six bounced from foot to foot.

All right! Nick said. Six? Green? Could we do a read-through?

They stood and read their lines, Six from her phone, and Green from practice last night.

Nice, good, that's fine! Nick said. When we film, Green, try maybe softening your voice, just a bit. It's sounding a bit too . . . insistent.

Huh, Green said. Like this? We're not taking a sideline, she said solemnly.

Better, Nick said. Just go in between that and that first go.

Got it, Green said. Thanks to Guthrie, she no longer took this kind of feedback personally.

They began rolling. Green and Six took their alternating lines with seriousness and warmth.

We're not taking a sideline, Green said.

We're putting ourselves at the center, Six said.

Sonus Sports has given us such a safe place to be ourselves.

As trans women, we can do our job without worrying about harassment.

We hope all trans women can find the same safety and support.

We need to keep asking big questions about gender and race in our sport.

In the meantime,

We'll see you on the court!

Cut! That was great, let me just play it back real quick.

Green grinned a quiet version of her Live Grin while Six jogged in place. This could not make the difference in her getting her spot. There was no way, she told herself.

Down on the court, Thom and Eric looked up at them, bored or even disdainful. Griffin was texting and Alan was setting a ball to himself. Even this disjointed arrangement looked like an ad for the coolness of sport, a boy band of breezy confidence.

Green knew that she and Six could never make as enchanting and legible a portrait. Such a comparison was futile. If Phil did his job, they will have co-opted Sonus's platform to advocate for the protection of hypersexualized trans women and sex workers and Asian femmes alike. They left no doubt where they stood. But by making such a literal appeal from the depths of their cis-bro sports league, they were also boxing themselves in.

Nick was back. It's good! he said. You two are really something.

Magnificent! Phil said, patting Green's hand.

So we can go? Six asked. Before Nick had finished saying *Yep,* she was sprinting across the court. Thank you! I'll see you later, sweetie!

Green's practice didn't start for another half hour. She waved back and turned to see Thom and Eric, still watching her. Was Thom just texting or was he taking a photo of her? She knew she would've been annoyed to the same intensity had they been ignoring her. She couldn't hate all men, not fully. She wouldn't survive her job if she did. But goodness, she hated these men.

###

She's just another influencer who pivots to being an activist when it's trending. It's not hard to only care about sex workers once a year!

God, how is Green handling it all? She must be exhausted. What an absolute shero!

Right? Is she just posting about this so she can deflect attention from the fact that she's playing in a superspreader sports tournament in the middle of a fucking pandemic?

Kind of funny watching everyone trying to one up each other with their soggy brain fry fog.

Losers like @bobababe59 trying to mooch off Six and Green's clout while posting videos where you're just saying random words. Please!

If you're looking for the he/him lookalikes with long hair but without the gender complex, @sixpointfive and @spearmintgreen are pretty dead ringers with pretty good LonelyFans, this is not #ad #notAd

It's so obvious which of our trans girls actually cares and which one's just saying something because her girlfriend said something so she doesn't look bad for being "neutral" LOL how do we get Green a better WAG?

Green being so over the top sad about the deaths of these three girls reeks of East Asian guilt

Medical transition is annoying but social transition is miserable honestly Six and Green chose the harder part

The transgendered community is solely responsible for the epidemic of narcissism in modern society.

Have a little empathy! It must be really hard to read the room when you're famous

Can't wait for them to finally reunite this Sunday!

Can't believe they gaslit the world with their elaborate fake dating show. I'm in awe.

###

When Six ran into the practice court, Czwartek was still jogging. Everyone except Sam. He was making this too easy for her. He was barely trotting. Was he injured? Pete nodded as she dropped her bag and joined the team.

Have a good time? he asked drily.

Yep, she called, speeding ahead to pass Sam.

When they began playing, Pete placed her with the starters, minus Alan and Sam. Six didn't relax. She still had to earn it. Pete wouldn't make it official for another hour.

After a few rallies, Alan returned from the shoot and took his spot over from Karl, fist-bumping Six.

How'd it go? she asked.

Good! They just needed me for that group clip you guys did and then some footage of me spiking but I didn't have any lines in that one.

Nice, I'm sure you did great, Six said. Across the net, Sam crossed his arms in a childish sulk.

With Alan back, Pete set up a new rotation to prepare against a hypothetical Aracaju.

When the ball reached the starters' side, James made the first touch, passing the ball to Dan, who set it to Alan, who spiked it easily. Six felt close. She would escape her peak-career purgatory.

When they huddled, Alan jogged to her and patted her fingers with his, the gesture surprisingly gentle. Dan patted her butt as if he'd been doing it all season. James tapped her tricep again, as if encouraging her before he set up to serve again. They touched her like she was one of the boys. Even if she hadn't played on their side of the net for much of the year, they all knew who she was and what could she do. Six felt her resolve grow. She rotated to her ideal base, middle front, just opposite of Sam.

The second stringers received the ball and attempted a kill that was dug by Dan, putting the starters out of system. Alan sprinted to set the ball to the center of the court. As it sailed above, Six approached. She felt Sam mirror her as she catapulted into the air and swung at the ball.

###

So far, Green and Six had tested negative. Just one more day before she'd get to kiss her silly girlfriend again. Tonight, Green was showing off her body to her via her phone, just two floors and some walls separating them now.

It was so affirming to look down at her body, there, right there, hers. She had worked for this feeling. She was there, in this room, in this tournament. She was doing her best, doing her job, in volleyball, as a human in this world, in grief, in the biggest week of her professional calendar, in a bubble. And she looked like this. Maybe it was the lighting that made her self-image so grounding. Maybe it was Six looking back at her so admiringly. Maybe it was denial.

In her red lacy halter and matching satin shorts, her contacts out and glasses cast aside, Green simply did not have the bandwidth to interrogate the complex composition of this feeling. She was shocked and alone and had no idea how to process what little she knew about Suzy and Bea and Clarisse. Someone had said Suzy and Bea and Clarisse had been susceptible because they were thin and beautiful and thus couldn't help but draw attention to themselves. Green knew that logic was awful but maybe it wasn't untrue in her own life. But she couldn't think about the other edge of the sword just now. She was trying to admire her figure in a floor-length closet mirror.

Green, you're so gorgeous. Six told her this because she could see Green trying to see herself and sensed it was a compliment Green would appreciate in this strange moment.

I know, right?

Everyone had basic needs at odd hours.

Green went on, That shoot was so weird! I'm glad we filmed our extra spot. Like that's a concrete positive message that'll go out into the world.

Six nodded, taking in the intensity of Green's expression. And Phil! I wonder if being an empty cliché of a person makes you happy.

Even without her glasses, Green could see Six shudder to herself. Also seated on her bed, she was massaging the calf of one leg, with the other splayed in front of her. Six wore mid-thigh running shorts and no top at all. I can't believe we're playing so soon, Green continued.

And that I'm starting!

And you're starting!

They had already gushed about it over dinner. They had gossiped about the shoot with the Curtis and Henry too but they had to talk about it again, just the two of them. She shouldn't have had to work so hard to get this spot. But Six felt so happy after Pete announced it.

I'm so proud of you, Green said again, to her girlfriend. To herself.

Thanks, beanie! Wait, are you going to do that panel with the sex worker collective?

Yep, Yemma confirmed it! We're on after my first match on Monday.

Wow, talk about range of motion.

Yeah, it's a lot, but Yemma's going to help me prepare and I'm talking to Guthrie about it before our show call on Sunday.

Oh, that's great! Six said. It was odd how they talked about this like it was any random collab, devoid of social or emotional gravitas. Green seemed to need this perspective, so Six went on, The fans will get to experience you in so many formats in those twenty-four hours.

Green wondered if the tone she heard in Six's voice was jealousy. She let Six's words echo in her mind and blinked. Right?

And you're gonna do so wonderfully, I know it.

Green blew a kiss. She still wasn't sure how to interpret Six's tone but couldn't afford for them to fight again. She needed them to stay strong. To diffuse the tension that maybe only existed in her mind, she asked, So, are you and Alan like besties now?

Wait, what?

I saw that photo he posted.

Huh?

On Instagraph?

Oh, I haven't seen it. I'll check tomorrow, I guess. Was it a good photo?

Yeah, it's really cute. He's kneeling at your feet but like, facing away so it's not like that. But you're both holding up peace signs.

Oh yeah, Alan asked Dan to take it after practice today.

You mean after Pete said you're taking Sam's spot?

Six's grimace barely masked the widest grin. Yeah.

And that was Alan's idea?

Six's mouth turned into a playful grin. She really had the most expressive face. I can't even be annoyed that he's so new anymore, because he was so excited for me. He was like, "I can't wait to play with you" and then "Wanna take a picture with me?" and then he took a couple selfies, basically right in front of Sam too—

He posted the selfie where you're holding the ball like you're setting and he's like squinting into the camera and leaning into you.

Wow, you really memorized these photos, huh? Six's mouth conveyed textbook bemusement, totally sincere.

I was just surprised to see them, Green said. How had she changed subjects to something *she* was jealous about? Also, he looks kinda gay next to you. Remember when he didn't know how to block?

I guess I've taught him a lot.

Like the Six-th sense?

Yeah, which includes how to be gay.

Right, it's not a gaydar. It's not a trans button. It's just full-on gay lesbo.

Six laughed. Gay lesbo?

I don't know, I'm delirious, I'm just saying stuff. Wait, did you see Yemma and Brent's message about that interview with *The Pacific*?

Uh, no?

So *The Pacific* wants to do a video package on us. They want to film it this weekend so it runs when the tournament starts.

Wait, really? *The Pacific*? Aren't we mad at them?

Well, yeah, they're the worst.

Until a month ago, the entirety of *The Pacific*'s trans coverage had come from one cis man who was gravely concerned over innocent cis teenagers being groomed by trans adults to take trans hormones. Yet, he had interviewed only one trans person in his five years reporting on the big trans question. Earlier this season, he got caught sending nudes to a teenager, trans of course, and was quickly fired.

So do you not want to do it? Six asked.

Well, Green hesitated, rubbing her neck. Brent and Yemma seem to think we should.

Six waited for Green to say she actually wanted to do it too.

And honestly, after this week, I kinda think we should.

So they want us to talk about the murders?

Well no, Brent and Yemma said they could make sure there's only one newsy tie-in. It'll mostly just about us and the tournament. You know, the groundbreaking trans athletes angle.

Six leaned her fist on her chin. But the murders are why they reached out last minute? Huh.

I—I guess? Green shrugged. Do you not want to do it?

I'm open to it. Just skeptical at the same time, you know?

Of course.

When do we have to confirm by?

The morning, basically.

That's considerate. Six leaned away from her phone. She sometimes wished Green were a little less tuned in. Maybe if she'd heard about it in the morning, she'd more amenable. Maybe if neither saw the request in time, they wouldn't have to deal with it at all.

Well—Green leaned forward conspiratorially—when they reached out to Brent and Yemma, the reporters did say something like, "We know *The Pacific*'s past coverage has sometimes disappointed the trans community and we hope that Six and Green would consider being part of turning over a new leaf."

Wow, a fresh start. How great. For *The Pacific*.

I know, Sixy. But it's *The Pacific*! Green breathed, remembering she usually had to egg Six on, encourage her to participate in the world with more vigor. Do you know the number of people who are going to see this? There's the video, the article with the photo spread, there's—

But this time, it won't be because two trans Asian girls made out on the court, it'll be because three trans Asian women were murdered.

Green sighed. I know, Six, I know. But it'll also be our first mainstream coverage not based on a viral video—

Six brought her camera to her face to zoom in on her raised eyebrow.

—and not just in the sports section or in the LGBTQ section or the Asian section. We'll get to talk about what we do and not just for Sonus. I know *The Pacific* has their own agenda. But we can have ours too.

Six repositioned her phone. I get it. I'm with you. Her smile looked a little sad. You didn't have to, but thanks for trying to convince me. It would be nice to honor Suzy and Bea and Clarisse, especially since no one else seems able to.

Wait, Walt did say something earlier today.

Wait, really?

Yeah, it was so weird. He came up to me and was just like, "Hey, I heard about the murders and it really sucks. A lot," and then he just kinda looked at me and I'm like, "Oh, okay, so you need me to lead this conversation for you. Yeah, nope." I just said, "Thanks," and then he ran away.

That is weird, Six agreed. But nice, I guess?

I guess. I just have no idea what inspired that weird allyship. Is he trying to lull me into a false sense of security so he can take my spot? Like he's my backup; we need each other but we're not going to be friends.

I know, babe. Good thinking, you stay sharp!

During the shoot, did you notice how even though Henry and Curtis are also getting the Sonus bonus this season, Phil only cared about us?

Six yawned. Yeah, he gave Thom and Eric a bro-y kind of hug, but—

—He gave us the beautiful girl treatment which, correct, but some people should really only be known through a screen.

Six flapped her arms. Honestly, talking to him made me a little paranoid.

About what?

What if Phil pressured Pete to start me? The way he winked when he mentioned wanting to watch me play . . . It was as if he knew it would happen. What if Pete's known he had to put me in and told Sam when we got here so that's why he hasn't even been trying?

Wow. Do you really think?

It's not unreasonable, right? Six put on a T-shirt and lay down. Like they're not going to invest extra money into me to just broadcast me standing around in the corner of the frame.

True, Green said from a child's pose now. But I wouldn't think about it that way. Even if Phil had anything to do with it, what are you supposed to do? It's your spot now. You just have to do your job and make sure Pete has no reason to sub you out.

You're right. I just wish I could know for sure that I earned it.

However you did it, you definitely did.

Six felt dizzy again. So besides *The Pacific* interview this weekend, we don't have to do anything else extra, do we?

Nope, just play. Unless. Green put on a slight pout and angled her camera. Now she was baby. Would you want to do that Fuck Your Exotic Fantasy panel with me? Not the whole thing but just the intro?

Six sighed, her face tired, but she didn't look away from the camera. Babe, I love you. But I just don't think I'll have the energy.

Green immediately leveled the camera with her face. She hadn't even gone into her pitch about how empowering it would be for the viewers tuning in worldwide to see them sitting side by side, supporting each other. She felt silly all of a sudden, like she was walking into a trap where everyone knew she had no idea what she was talking about. Of course Six didn't want to put herself in the crosshairs. Green's eyes began to water. Of course, babe. I understand.

Thanks for asking me. You know I'm here to support you.

Green thought Six's expression looked genuinely encouraging. She breathed.

Six wondered if it was a good idea for Green to be taking on roles she hadn't necessarily been preparing for. She thought about saying something, but she was so tired, she knew she'd mess it up.

I'm handling all this right, right? Green asked. Like, it's hard but also, I don't know when we're going to get an opportunity like this again. Now's our time, right? For us. For all of us.

We're all doing our best, Gweenie. I'm genuinely so proud of you.

You mean it?

Six produced a rare Live Grin. I love you and I wouldn't fake shit for you.

Not even the week of a tournament? Green's eyes shone bright, her focus line-drive sharp even at this hour.

Not when the white people are out there murdering our sisters and getting away with it.

Green turned away from her camera and dragged her palm down her face. She couldn't take in what Six had just said. They said good night.

###

Green didn't mention that *The Pacific* assigned the story to one white trans man and one cis (queer?) Asian woman. This was supposed to be the first time perspectives "from the trans community" were being centered in the legacy publication's history. But these people? When average-heighted Fritz and Tricia (really, even their names) looked up at them when they shook hands in the Sonus arena lobby, their zealous expressions were too wanting of Six and Green. They were so desperate to be the right people to interview them, it made them inherently ill-equipped for the job. Six was on guard immediately.

It had been too long a week for two people to ask what her pronouns were and encourage her to totally let them know if they did anything that made either of them uncomfortable. Fritz's voice, so queer and impersonally chipper, did not create a safe space for Six. Her body was in shock. After practicing with the starters the past few days, she was so sore, she realized how little she'd demanded of her body from the other side of the net. She had nothing left for this.

The Pacific had coordinated with Phil to begin filming at

the end of Regalado's practice so they could capture Green's team playing in the background of the shot. After they left the court, they all walked down the hallway and Six gave an intro to the tournament. Tricia asked Green about the pandemic and their Instagraph Live show. In the gym, Tricia asked about their seasons and Six told her and Fritz how thankful they were to have stayed healthy to get to practice and compete at all.

Perhaps two of these nine minutes made the final cut.

Fritz asked, As trans athletes, how does it feel playing on men's sports teams? From behind the camera, he made an exaggeratedly apologetic face.

Green looked to Six, who squeezed her hand. She had given less refined versions of this answer over the years but now, with all her media experience, she could produce an answer that would maximize clicks and humanize trans women to the world. Hardly inhaling, her voice emerged steady.

And on it went. Tricia's next question began, "As Asian women . . ." They filmed more B-roll of Six and Green squatting and whirring ropes in agitated waves. Before the shoot began, Green had squeezed Six's hand. As they passed each other on and off camera, they passed the squeeze back and forth. Six wondered if Fritz or Tricia would remark upon this nonverbal gesture in their little blog post.

While the crew set up in the courtyard, Green reapplied shimmer to Six's browbones with such ferocity that Six's eyeballs buzzed. She had to keep it together. If Tricia noted a moment of weakness, the public might think Six's team was working her too hard and her team would blame her for negative press.

As they walked beneath the unfiltered sun, Tricia asked

if they wanted to talk about the murders at all. No pressure, of course.

Green lifted her jaw to catch the light and infused her voice with great seriousness. Six and I have been just devastated. It's been difficult processing this from within this COVIS bubble. But we hope that by playing on, we can model the kind of resilience our community has always found in times like these. Green performed their requisite privilege checking before talking about building new interest in volleyball for young kids so that in ten, fifteen years, leagues would become inclusive by default and no longer as a reaction. She talked about wanting to win. For Suzy, Bea, and Clarisse, of course.

Meaning, you want to beat your girlfriend again? Fritz asked.

Six let out a laugh. She didn't want to be here, but couldn't help catching the light at every shift of her torso and neck. Radiating beauty was so automatic at this point that no one would think to ask if she needed time to curl up into a ball and cry or sleep. But maybe even this internal conflict would make a moving story for an interview in a few years' time. Yeah, Fritz, she said. She absolutely does. But we'll see about that. Six gave an effervescent wink directly to the camera, the gesture casual and provoking, glib and sexy and adorable and undeniably winsome.

###

Walt had practice in six hours but she was suffering from anguish. She let out the briefest wail. Lying on her hotel bed, she tried to fling her arm behind her with a feminine flourish of the wrist. Her hand hit the headboard with a pathetic slump. Her too-long fingers uncurled dramatically from her phone, which fell onto the floor.

She would need much more than six hours to acquire enough coordination or finesse to change the trajectory of her Sonus Tournament. She'd read an essay about how trans women could bend time but maybe she didn't have it in her to do it. Maybe she was so far off, she hadn't even understood the essay.

She supposed it didn't really matter if she showed up to the court a haggard zombie. Green would start regardless. She was perfect; she'd earned it. Walt was a perpetual second stringer. She would have to wait her turn. From being the backup setter in high school varsity, NCAL, and now Regalado, she'd been lucky enough to keep finding coaches who wanted to sign her, but never enough to be wanted on game day. She had to be more confident, more like Green. Her body was supposed to be more than a vessel, but a portal, its whole impossibly too much and not enough at the same time. She knew she could be pretty but she wanted more than a hypothetical. She wanted to be free from shame.

She couldn't help wondering if Green's look of incredulity at her talking about the murders was more than a reaction to her ugliness. Maybe Green couldn't fathom that the murders of beautiful women had anything to do with her. Him. She had hoped it might be a pivotal moment of connection that they'd remember as the moment they became friends: the moment

Green looked at Walt and saw a she in hiding. How delusional. Green was never going to envelop her in a conspiratorial hug.

She couldn't fall asleep smothered by doubt. She'd have to spend another night trying to distinguish between the feeling and fact of dysphoria. She supposed this was a prerequisite stage for all trans people. She groaned into a pillow and something guaranteed not to help: she regarded that ruthless mirror. She would never be original. She couldn't fix the breadth of her too-wide shoulders or her too-deep voice. She already shaved her legs for functional reasons. But what she really wanted was to sculpt her brows for Sonus television the way she sculpted them when she was alone.

But she'd never have to worry about being on camera. She'd never have Green's fast twitch muscles. She would never be good enough or famous enough or woman enough to be a starting setter. Her 24k followers put her in the 87th percentile of Instagraph users, but she still wasn't famous enough to know people outside her field. There was no trans or even cis queer influencer friend with whom she could reminisce wistfully, Ahh, remember when we had the privilege of being obscure? She had signed up for the trans train reluctantly and too late and too privately. At the same time, she was just famous enough where making friends with common strangers was always risky. How honest could she be about herself without revealing that she was a professional athlete? Walt was paid so well but couldn't afford what she most wanted to buy. There was no two-day shipping to feel authentically and safely herself anywhere without losing it all. When she hit her first growth spurt, she was sorted as ungainly, which only made her feel dorky and awkward. She learned to live with discomfort in her own skin. That sophomore semester in college, she played Token Asian Friend with that all-white group of twinks till someone posted a group picture where they all looked photogenic and her eyes were splotchy and mouth agape. She stopped responding to the group chat, and they never asked where she'd gone.

Watching Six and Green navigate the last forty-eight hours only made her scared. Even if she had a friend to guide her, if she received half of the negative attention they did, she would collapse. Maybe the fans weren't wrong but they were all so mean about it! Walt could handle the boyish kind of brusque, brutish meanness. Her colleagues were unsubtle but manageable. But the queer varietals of clever backhands would be fatal.

So instead, back home Walt mostly had anonymous sex with horny man-dudes and repressed eggs she'd met on apps. She'd made profiles where she was a faceless gay man with butt cheeks. She'd made profiles displaying her perfect eyebrows and the promise of submissive femininity. She'd entered prissy apartments and disgusting hovels. She played sub and she also heard things like, I didn't expect you to feel so strong, so powerful, as if they were surprised that the naked torso they'd thumbed knew how to wield its body. Once, when she wasn't thinking, she responded, Did you expect me to be delicate because I'm Asian or because I'm a girl? She realized she should've left when he wasn't even offended. Sometimes a hookup made her feel good for a few minutes but they all left her feeling worse. Tonight, there was no one to help her jostle sensations around. She was on her own.

She looked again at the photos of the victims she'd saved on her phone. They were so beautiful. Walt was stricken, shocked, so sad they were gone. Murdered. She knew she didn't know them and knew that staring at these photos and scrolling through Suzy's and Clarisse's Instagraphs was a perverse voyeurism. But she was a closeted pre-op trans girl playing man sport. She was already deeply unwell. So she let herself piece together a montage of the lives these women, these distant sisters, had led.

Suzy had been a graphic designer who reminded her 683 followers that she was open to commissions nearly every other post. Clarisse posted photos of herself only with other people—her boyfriend, who hadn't posted in three weeks; her friends, with whom she clinked glasses in tiny clips that kept looping, the toast perpetually arriving but the first sip always in the distance. Bea was perhaps the most beautiful of them all. Her account was made private, probably by a loved one, shortly after the death and Walt hadn't found it in time. But photos of her had begun trickling onto a public In Memoriam page. It wasn't just her tastefully developed breasts and hourglass figure, which Walt admired with equal parts envy and guilt. It was the demure pout of her lips and surprised look in her eyes that was so genuine, so vulnerable, Walt couldn't imagine anyone but the most intimate friend or lover had captured these photos. She tried again to recreate one of her poses: one hip turned just slightly to the camera, her knees and ankles squeezed tight, and above, her chest and shoulders rotated the opposite way, accentuating a tiny but soft-looking waist in the middle.

The mirror didn't lie this time either. It showed Walt lowering her weak-looking chin and looked up, trying to act surprised at her own image. Walt had a nice butt but her hip bones made it look lumpy instead of luscious. Walt's mouth looked both stiff and flaccid, awkward rather than sexy. She knew she shouldn't have tried to recreate it in this state. Trying to feel more feminine while feeling dysphoric usually only made her feel more dysphoric. She knew trans girls could have martini glass torsos with narrow hips. But she didn't want to be one of those girls. She knew not having long hair or not ingesting testosterone-blockers didn't make her less of a woman. But they did make her less of the woman that she wanted to be.

As she scoured the newsfeeds for updates on the case, she saw a quickly materializing vigil in Alpharetta in two days, just before the tournament would start. She imagined escaping the bubble to fly out before returning in time to sit on the bench, just in case Green couldn't play. An impossible fantasy.

She hadn't been able to find any confirmation that the three of them had known each other. If they had no untraced connection, she wondered how they had all wound up together that night. The internet had plenty of ideas. She imagined them meeting for a girls' night out, maybe a few blocks away, before strolling through Alpharetta's downtown to the hotel. She considered how she'd probably look, wearing her usual fitted sweatsuit over neon-blue striped sneakers. She'd read as tall and athletic. But her unremarkable bone structure would also make her fade into the background. She felt nauseated realizing she was worried she wasn't hot enough to be even considered a target.

She knew she couldn't be trans and safeguard her low tolerance for being perceived. Maybe if she was brave enough to feel scared, she could feel a part of something. She wondered if Suzy, Bea, and Clarisse had felt scared that night. Walt was scared of being found out. She was scared of being even more scared. She was scared of not knowing if anyone would care to notice she was there, waiting, this whole time, ever since she'd known, ever since she realized she didn't have so much a choice as much as she had a decision. She'd decided volleyball.

And three years later, her loftiest childhood dream, from before she knew, presented itself. She would become a professional volleyball player, and with Regalado, the team that had managed to snag Green. Walt had to take the opportunity to breathe the same air as her. But over the course of four seasons, she had realized she'd gotten too comfortable hiding in Green's shadow. But if Green didn't transfer or move, Walt wasn't sure where she could go. It's not like other coaches had seen her play enough to want to poach her. She felt stuck, though at least she was alive.

Walt tossed her comforter in the air and turned off the lights. While she couldn't yet pervert the gender regime, she could check the forum. She plopped onto her back and brought the bright light an inch from her retinas. There were 261 new messages across eight threads. She scrolled through the forums that usually had regular activity—photo boost, 'mones and knives, throwing a fit, fucking and dating, intros—and the newsier forums—{TW: anti-trans violence, whorephobia, racism}, the Alpharetta Murders 2021, Big House Season 39: Candice, Tracking the Bathroom Bills. Six and Green became the subject of a thread when that inane video of them making out after the final last year had gone viral, but thankfully this was a fairly sports-averse community. Walt's eyes glazed at her avatar. On this anonymous forum, everyone had random objects or celebrity photos or animated characters. This rounded image of Senna, Walt's favorite anime character with the big eyes and ten eyelashes, was the closest anyone knew her as her.

She clicked on "Alpharetta Murders 2021," where one of the power users, @SuperCold (87,399 posts) had the most recent post: "Ladies, let's be mindful of how we're passing judgments on their desirability under the cis gaze. Hotness is not a value-neutral word." She always knew what to say. Walt wondered what @SuperCold looked like in real life. Maybe she could help her figure out what to do next. She knew she was a liberal subject with some agency to activate but she just needed someone to tell her how.

###

If you're in Chicago and need cupping to get those sexy bruises like Six, DM @BurningOrbsChicago for an appt I'll make sure you have a happy ending

They're really going in on this live. Like this is so deep.

Are they actually a good couple or do they just look good on instagraph?

I can't believe they're broadcasting from the same time and place.

I know trans girls are always whining about being the least represented, most oppressed type of tranny but like, Six and Green cancel all those complaints out.

But with TWO camera angles tho. Green does not have a bad side at all does she?

Yay! No COVIS for our babies!

@sixsosweet who's your voice coach?

This little speech by Green is gonna make me hurl, it's so CANNED! She needs to fire her speechwriter and just hire an acting coach!

Every type of tranny thinks they're the most oppressed tranny. Last month it was the afab enbies and next month it'll be the generic genderfluid fuckers.

People, Six and Green are FAKE DATING. Six is STRAIGHT. He has a GIRLFRIEND! It's ME! I'm his GIRLFRIEND!

Still seems kinda risky . . . just because they're negative from a test two days ago doesn't mean they can't still be incubating the virus.

Wait I thought Six was genderfluid. Since they haven't medically transitioned, wouldn't it be easier if they just identified as a non-binary they-thembo or whatever?

Did anyone see Green on that panel last night? Can't believe she's streaming her face so soon after that embarrassment.

Six seems really shaken by this. We love you Six! You're so strong!

Well, not everyone accesses womanhood via knives and pills. Some girls find it within.

No! I missed the first three minutes. They must've shadowbanned them.

How is @badboybryan here every week? Report @badboybryan!!!!

So you're saying Six and Green are more woman than those who have suffered under knife and pill to be? What is wrong with you?

Wait @transaretrans what did Green say? Was it recorded?

Saying athletes are famous because of their follower count is a tautology!

They can't still be crying about this nearly a week later, can they?

Yeah, we should be talking about how taut that body is!

Even if I buy the VIP pass and get to meet them I won't have anyone to film them hugging me and I'll be too hysterical to remember a second of it

Yes Six you take in those deep breaths. Let that oxygen flow through every sexy organ you possess!

Green was just reading from 2.5 wave feminism bullets about how sex work is work. She added nothing to the convo besides followers clogging the stream

How are they supposed to play tomorrow if they're emotionally unstable like this?

Six is the best girlfriend, if she ever patted me on the back like that, all my core wounds would heal immediately

If they don't start talking about how practice has been going, I'm logging off.

Come on, Six HAS to be starting!

Is Six wiping tears or keeping Green's makeup intact?

Ok then log off @spikycity! Nobody asked you to be here!

Are we actually just gonna sit here til they make their little announcement? Yeah fucking right

BOTH @minteyhoney BOTH!

Ugh, of course, Green has to fix Six's makeup, Six has no idea what she's doing

Glad the arena's beautiful! Can't wait to see it @everyourgreen

Are you finally going to film a vlog with Curtis?!

Stop trying to make trans people out to be special unicorns @transaretrans. We're only resilient because cis straight people like you exist

Kind of nefarious how Six and Green are able to keep hitting ball like robots in a crisis

Omg! I knew it! SIX IS STARTING! FINALLY!

Media literacy is so broken, did none of you read that investigation

Yeah, it must be so hard to work when you're a literal millionaire

showing how Six and Green were planted by the Chinese engagement overlords to hack American attention

Now I'm literally crying! After such a long season, I'm so fucking proud of you @sixsosweet ! You deserve this, you deserve the world

and farm our user data and project testosterone in our eyeballs

I hope their publicist gets a monster bonus when this is all over

making us all aggressively horny so that we'll pay for

A rematch of Six and Green on the court this tournament? What did we do to deserve this blessing??

Are they even focused on this tournament? Like I get them processing the murders and whatnot but why are they doing it on Live? If I were them, I would've just skipped this week.

Well, only if they both make it to the final again

I can just tell there's so much pain and grief behind Green's smile

I feel like insisting they're girls so much reminds you they're not

Are we going to talk about how Six booted Sam? I hope Sam takes his spot back.

It seems kinda creepy how Six and Alan are friends doesn't it?

I get they're trying to not be erased but I feel like all these jokes are participating in essentializing their own gender. How sad

Yeah @tim3290 I feel like Six is grooming an innocent kid

Poor Six, she never talks about her parents or her family. I wonder if her refugee parents disowned her because she was trans or chose a career in sports. Bet they're sorry now

Did you see Czwartek's announcement? Sam's taking the tournament off to recover from an injury.

Wait, is Alan trans?

@tim3290 do you think Six bullied the league into getting their coach to let Six start?

Yooo @everyourgreen long time remember when we were chem lab partners and now look at you! Actually playing ball! Let's catch up sometime! haha

Six loves her parents, have you not seen the old tapes of them cheering her on at all her NCAL games?

Isn't it funny how Czwartek needed to hit their diversity quotient and there was Six, ready to boot off the team's more talented blocker? I hate woke politics, grow up you babies

Branding is a shiny house of smoke screen mirrors that incentivizes girls to bifurcate our identities at unsustainable speeds of self-dissonance, leading to

There's no such thing as trans people @transaretrans! What nonsense!

Why did Czwartek lie? Sam announced he's taking time to focus on his mental health

no @theory4babes houses always depreciate over time, but even if you get canceled, your personal brand can only ever appreciate and as soon as you accept that, you'd stop being poor!

There's something in Six's face, like she's not winking but it's almost like she is!

But it's never too late to divest from self-image, seduce the landlord, and abolish the department of homeland insecurity

Yeah @rickyyyyyy_fanclub there is! It makes me wonder, what else does she know?!

###

KILL

THE MORNING OF HER RETURN TO THE LINEUP, SIX woke with a headache. She couldn't believe she was going to play again. Maybe Sonus had bullied Pete into putting on the show their ads had promised viewers all year. Maybe Sam wasn't injured or taking care of his mental health. Maybe she would never know if she'd earned any of it on her own ever again. She could never undo becoming famous. But volleyball still meant so much to her. And everyone was waiting.

Now a week after the murders, she'd let herself cry for a few minutes before SpaceTiming Green, who was still thrilled at her own performance on Live last night. She had managed to cry on camera. Green's image shimmered at the prospect of the Sonus video releasing today and *The Pacific* package tomorrow. Six was genuinely happy for her. She didn't mention her headache, which accompanied her through the morning, from hotel breakfast to the arena. It seemed to ebb in intensity but she was paying too much attention to it to be sure. Maybe she had actually willed it away. Maybe it had never been there at all. She decided gaslighting herself would be more effective than panicking.

Most days, work helped her focus her energy and channel it through the ball. But during warm-up, she felt nothing. She managed to eye the ball adequately enough and no one seemed to notice. Sam sat out and Pete didn't take her off the lineup. Maybe there was nothing to notice. Six was a girl who knew when to be a distressed damsel and when to suffer in solitude. But could she really win an entire game like this?

Alan usually got pre-game zoomies but this was the first time Six could appreciate it as an equal teammate, not just a resentful bench hag. As she watched the tiny pulsing of his legs between every drill, through Pete's pep talk, and back to the locker room, she found herself calmed by his jitters. His energy swapped nerves for real excitement. As he frantically tapped his thighs beside her, she felt her headache dull. For sure this time. The clanging within her skull morphed into a pleasant thrum. She could work with this.

And then it was time. They were playing her old team, La Spezia. As Czwartek took the private stairs up two flights to enter the arena, Six felt an unfamiliar hum in her stomach as she thought about the show she was meant to put on. For what sports arena was not also a theater?

They could hear the buzz of the crowd taking their seats, passing around snacks they would theoretically eat quickly before re-masking. The rest of the team was starting to match

Alan's physicality. Shoulders loosened through near-violent arm swings, hands slapped back and forth so that fingers would caress that soft touch. And absently, Six joined them in gentle jump squats. The hallway floor wasn't sprung but it felt good to feel her brain bounce in her skull, just a bit.

A Sonus PA raised his hand and the loose clump of players slicked into a neat line.

Number 9 from Czwartek, we have middle blocker James Akbari!

Charlie held the door open as James trotted through, one arm already raised in a wave. The audience began clapping. Then Dan, Alan, Igor, and Kenny. Then:

And next, Number 6, give it up for middle blocker Six!

There was only the open door in front of her now. She burst through, picking up her knees to disguise her deliberate pace. The lights slammed in her face and awoke something carnal in her. From her ankles to her retinas, her body remembered what to do. When she swished down the last step, she waved in acknowledgment of the loud roar. She knew it didn't just sound louder because she was inside of it. The packed arena was louder for her.

And then they brought on Emir, the libero, and Six was out of the spotlight. She still couldn't see but felt it. She turned around. She hopped forward and back, side to side, alternating feet. She turned around again. Her headache was gone. In its absence, total clarity. All it took was for her to swim in that dazzle of lights again. Being the center of attention wasn't a toxin; it was an overdue therapeutic intervention. A jolt of pressure that brought Six back to life. Behind her, Alan set a ball, and without thinking, Six turned over her shoulder and felt that crackle on her forearms as she passed it back in the most ravishing arc.

And before she knew it, they were up two sets to none. She loved the way the game made time dissolve. Here's how the commentators called the conclusion of the match:

And La Spezia calls for a challenge! Whether they got a touch off the block or not, it's all academic at this point. It would take a disaster for Czwartek to lose the match. While we wait, let's talk about Six's comeback performance. Tanner, what stands out to you?

Well, Rudy, at twenty-seven, Six is probably near the height of her physical capabilities as a player. She made a risky decision switching teams at this stage of her career with Czwartek already having two incredible middle blockers before she joined. Six has looked so sharp in practice this week and it's incredible seeing her rise to the occasion and compete like she hasn't spent all season on that bench.

She has definitely impressed so far. She's been up against her old teammates who know all of her tricks. La Spezia's only ranked eleventh but she was on that silver-medal-winning team last year.

And to be clear, Rudy, La Spezia was practicing so much better this week, they just haven't been able to keep up with number two, Czwartek.

And there was no touch! Czwartek keeps the point and we'll go to our first match point of the tournament. Tanner, the computer doesn't lie.

The computer doesn't lie! Czwartek's up 24–16 on a 7–2 run, so they have seven chances to take this first match and get one step closer to the finals. Kenny may have scored two aces out of those seven points but it's Alan, the youngest starting member of this dominant team, who's never looked steadier in his first season than he has today.

Part of being young is you're still finding your rhythm as a pro. You're playing at a faster pace, you're getting new coaching. And he's actually changed his pre-serve throughout this season. Every player has his set number of dribbles and moves they've built to set up that the serve the way he likes it. Here he goes.

That was 108 kilometers an hour, just a floater but it's already got La Spezia out of system.

Whoa, and a wild swing from Hamilton, so that's a free ball for Czwartek, and Humphries with just a gorgeous set! And it's over! Six gets it done in a match fitting her return! Six wins the first match of the Sonus Tournament for Czwartek!

Wow, what a beautiful moment. She's had to have been so frustrated waiting all season for her chance but today, she hasn't been subbed out once. Thirteen blocks and six attacks ties her with Alan for the most points this match.

But really, because Six is a middle and not a hitter, I would say her points count even more. Even though she's been around for so long, you still would've forgiven her if she'd looked a little tentative today. But what a display of calm precision for Czwartek.

Tanner, you can hear the roar of this crowd. Maybe half

of them wanted La Spezia to rebound from this but all of them are just so hyped by this amazing showing from Czwartek. If this is the energy the crowd is showing for a match in pool play, I can't imagine what it'll sound like for the finals.

Rudy, if you've been commentating to empty arenas all year, you can just say that.

Haha! And you haven't?

No, I've only been commentating with you.

And we're going to take a look at this special announcement from league sponsor Sonus.

Wow, what a powerful message, what splendid ambassadors for the sport.

Rudy, I played with Green back in the day—you know, my last season. And to see her speaking up about such an important issue on this stage is just so inspiring to see.

And here's Carly Owens, on the floor with Czwartek's star player of the match, Six.

Six, congratulations on such a commanding return to the lineup. And thank you so much for your inspiring message. How are you feeling right now?

Well, Carly, honestly, it's been a tough season. I've been doubting myself a lot. I woke up with just the worst headache this morning but just getting to play on this world stage again—who knew a little set and spike would be the cure? Maybe my headache was just nerves. Maybe it's grief. It's been a lot to process this past week. I was thinking about Green and wishing she could be there today, but of course she has her own game later. I remembered this is how we've been doing this. We know we're there for each other. I felt both so rooted in my body and also like I could spill out my skin. Volleyball is magic and I'm so honored it flows through me.

###

I can't believe she said, "We're putting ourselves at the center." Some people have no self-awareness

I can't believe she said, "Volleyball is magic and I'm so honored it flows through me." She's so embarrassing

I'm so mad I missed Six's first game back but I had to work a double, vinmo @minteyhoney to help pay last month's rent

If you don't post about these murders you are complicit in the future deaths of all trans and/or Asian people.

Six and Green really heard about last week and saw an opportunity huh?

What happened to locker room reporting? Sonus must be so broke.

"Volleyball is magic and I'm so honored it flows through me" I felt that in my sacrum someone hand me a tissue!

Ok, that fluff piece was camp but there are bigger problems right? If they pass the bathroom ban, I'll never get to pee next to Green! We must organize!

How do I bottle the noise from the arena so I can shoot it up next winter when COVIS comes back?

Volleyball does support Asian trans women! It gets better, capitalist queers!

The last thing we need is more skinny trans girls being like, "Ooh skinny trans girl representation"

If you don't stop obsessing over Six and Green and start

obsessing about the bathroom bans and medical bans you are enabling your own bodily oppression by fascism!

I'll give you Green but name a single part of Six's body that isn't juicy

What hotel are the athletes staying at?

Six being so confident about not taking hrt gave me the confidence to finally stab myself in the thigh

Aren't all Asian men 5'7"? How is Six basically 7 feet tall?

Who needs beta blockers, put the girls on vball so they can channel their little mental calculations towards ball smacking

Like if you know Six and Green are real women because their bodies wouldn't be policed like this if they were boys

Is Six actually hot or is she just tall?

Love to see trans people coming for trans influencers profiting off of three women's murders. That's right girls, we tear each other down!

###

Like Czwartek, Regalado won their first match against Aracaju. Luckily, the pool play point system still gave room for Aracaju to advance to the finals. Green shrugged apologetically before hugging Henry and Curtis across the net. Curtis held Green's wrists and winked theatrically. Henry's hand on her waist was tender even in its brief touch. Over her shoulder, Walt crept near the back of the line, staring at her. He smiled, sheepishly. So weird.

From her hotel bed, Green turned on her knee-high compression booties and checked her socials. Yemma and Brent had made sure that the Sonus video cross-posted to her and Six's accounts when it was released at the end of Six's game.

This was the highest engagement Green had ever seen. At 857k followers, she had only 60k fewer than Six, the closest she had been in years. She wanted to win at this tiny game in her mind, even if it only lasted a few hours. Green returned to the familiar comfort of her grid, a scrapbook of her beautiful face. As she scrolled through her latest comments, she remembered her therapist and Yemma's advice to not get stuck on the negative ones. She chose to ignore them, them being her therapist and Yemma.

When a girl's beauty and wealth were public, haters were inevitable. It wasn't worth reporting comments—she would never get through them all. In this era of routine online humiliation, everyone knew that trying to draw attention away from something only drew more attention to it. Let the harassment and hate speech and misplaced criticisms get lost in the swirl of hearts and stars and other imagistic expressions of their fans' adulation.

She did read the semi-coherent essays citing quotes she'd given years ago to prove she couldn't be trusted. Yemma disagreed but Green believed understanding the range of projections randos placed on her could only help her reassert control.

Today, the haters accused her of profiting from this horrible, violent incident. It was ridiculous. She posted in her stories that she would double any (inconsequential) speakers' fees and donate them to mutual aid collectives. Would there be an eventual return on this pro bono investment into establishing herself as a thought leader on Asian American and transgender issues? Activists couldn't work for free forever. Surely, the fact that she had to think about these optics made her a better person than someone who just hit post, took the cash, and moved on.

In a roundabout way, each comment motivated her to keep trailblazing. There was nothing like that eternally renewable resource: spite. Even before the murders, she had so many ideas. Anything could fail but anything could succeed. If no one bought the memoir she wanted someone to ghostwrite, maybe the auto-tuned dance track she might record would become the latest viral challenge. If the cameo on a network drama didn't blip on the cultural radar, maybe a reality show about the sundry dramas of West Coast WAGs would be the latest streaming phenomenon. The world deserved a celebrity like her, for, when had they ever had one like her?

For now, she wanted to let other girls know that it was okay to be sad, that it was necessary to ask for more, that they must not cower in fear. Bea had been the first Asian person and first trans woman president of the *Radford Law Review*. When Green had read her editors' admiring obituaries, she wondered which ones had secretly undermined Bea's tenure. Right-wing pundits already criticized Clarisse for being unemployed while dropping $100 at the nail salon. If only they knew how much work it took girls like her to create a presence that deflected judgment. And even with such armor, any attention was a potential threat. But the very real risk of aggressive violence must not—Green hoped *The Pacific* wouldn't edit this out—diminish their lives any more than it already did. They must keep taking up space.

Green went to Six's page and looked at the mostly nice comments below her post sharing the identical video file. Maybe if Green were ugly, the differences in their treatment would be heightened, but also, Six might take her insecurities more seriously. Being pretty was a comorbidity. If she told Six about her observations now, Six would just remind her that the algorithm was designed to make Green mad, that Green should just stop reading, as if that original suggestion would cure Green of whatever this was called.

###

@everyourgreen Why don't you try doing an actual job that actually uses your body? I wanna see you running around a freezing factory shoving packets of random shit into boxes with no pee break and try telling us to be unapologetic about taking up space.

I wanna say the Pacific fumbled it, but Six and Green agreed to film a glorified workout video that all but tells me I should be ashamed I don't do enough sit ups.

Is Green eating her greens? She's looking a little gaunt

Congratulations you've just won a new smile beautiful please claim your boob new job home ponytail improvement face lift DM coupon for more info

Did no one tell Green you can't have four media events four days in a row? The Fuck Your Exotic Fantasy panel, another episode of Six and Green, the Sonus video statement, and now the Pacific?

God, Green looks so glamorous when her face gets emaciated like this

Ingrained male socialization has her forgetting what happens when women are overexposed

But don't you see how these influencers are already too late?

Green's asking people to show up? Where? How? Isn't she at a fucking sports tournament? Are we going to abolish the police one bag-checking rent-a-cop at a time?

How much do we think they got paid for that Pacific exclusive interview?

What if Green just did what she's telling us to do and didn't make a fuss about trying to convince us to do it with her?

You think the most reputable magazine in the country pays its profile subjects? What's it like being ignorant?

I hate that I hate read all these comments. How do I get the app to just show me the nice ones?

Remember how Six flew out to see Green in the third month of the pandemic while the rest of us were still in quarantine?

Imagine being as wealthy as Green and stopping your transition at designer dresses, laser hair removal, and mani-pedis. Imagine how perky the titties, how prissy the pussy she could have sculpted, what a waste.

Kind of sad how desperately Green wants to be perceived and she looks for that feeling in precisely the worst place possible: the online.

Dude, you can't just teach the algorithm, you have to become the algorithm.

###

Walt watched the video for at least the thirtieth time since she'd gotten to her hotel room. She'd seen it on Green's page, on Six's, and on Sonus's. She hadn't moved in two hours.

She also hadn't meant to let the video loop so many times but she couldn't help being transfixed. They were so convincing and soothing, it almost made her feel better doing nothing about anything. She'd spent the afternoon warming up to watch Green set up plays she could never dream of. Off the court, she kept refreshing the news for updates from Alpharetta. The police had released grainy security footage from the hotel. She tried to channel her pent-up energy toward hating the fuzzy murderer but it didn't work. It was just exhausting.

Walt's job was restricting her womanhood in too many ways. The livestreamed memorial service was during their first game, so now she had to wait for someone to upload the feed online. Not that watching the recording all alone would make her feel any better. If she couldn't even psych herself up to enter the chat during the livestream, when would she ever get the chance to become the woman she wanted to be? And even if her boss gave her five pity minutes of pool play game time, the camera would turn away from the court to watch Green drink water. Maybe she needed more than her summer break.

She still hadn't posted on the forum. A cascading livestream chat felt low-stakes but a forum post was permanent. It was the same inertia that kept her phone in her hand with the video still looping. She'd stopped taking in the image or noises. Her hand went slack and her phone clattered against her bedside table. Hearing Green and Six's voice separated from their image broke the spell. She wiped her sweaty hands on her oddly dry thighs and reached down for her link to society.

Ugh, she whined aloud in the high-pitched, squealish voice only anonymous strangers had heard from her. Green invited you to do it, so just do it, she thought. Okay, she said aloud now, Green literally told her followers to do it. You're on the same team as her, so you follow her, so it's not a big deal. Just do it.

She picked up her phone, tapped the *share* button and resized the thumbnail. She added some emojis (bro hands raised, masculine exclamation points) and the main hashtag (#SonusForAll) and shared it.

Walt sighed. It was 1:19 a.m., a totally casual time to be online. Before she could wait for any engagement, she switched to the forum. She really should sleep but there were a dozen new posts in the Six and Green thread. *The Pacific* had posted a nine-minute video profiling them. Two hours ago. She groaned even louder this time. Even if it was bad, she suspected it would still hypnotize her for another hour. At least Regalado didn't have practice till the afternoon again. She remembered seeing the camera crew following them around the arena just the other day. She wasn't hoping she would see herself literally but hoped she might see herself figuratively. Alas, even in the video thumbnail, Six and Green radiated overwhelming star power. She was beyond brain-dead but awake enough to realize she would not see herself at all.

###

A few floors and rooms away, he (@transaretrans, 85k followers) logged into his second backup fake account. The first backup had already been hacked, so he had to be sure. Seated at his cheap hotel room desk in a pair of boxers and a ratty Sonus tee, his focus was sharp. Sonus had sent a press kit to the entire league, so he had access to this slapdash self-aggrandizing sloppy shit of a video. He lowered the bit rate just slightly to create the loss in quality inevitable in an anonymous source (him) sending this anonymous account (also him) the file. He flipped it upside down and added a tiny watermark in the corner. In front of the white fluorescent light of the desk lamp, he wrote a caption:

> Did you see the opening match of the Sonus Volleyball tournament? Who was playing for Czwartek? Who wasn't?
>
> Observe now this video, released today by Sonus. What exactly are they trying to communicate—that they exist? That they insist on being women, yet get to refuse at the same time? That they've managed to game the

> system and take away the most elite jobs from thousands of talented young men? That they feel a sense of duty to "the community" and make better money than any of us will ever know?
>
> We have a big update coming later this week. #transaretrans

He posted it.

He knew that doing so was making his target public. Yesterday's half-assed post about a vlogger who made awkward videos about how trans people should be written about in books had been filler. His caption had read, "What makes anyone think they should decide what should be in trans books?" Both the vlogger's account and @transaretrans had seen an uptick in new subscribers. It wasn't engagement baiting. It was virtual symbiosis to nurture the ecology of those committed to protecting the material realities for real transgender people.

Reading that profile in *The Pacific* had made him dead certain. Six and Green spoke so complacently but hadn't realized their politics had gone astray. His plan would help Six and Green course correct and protect trans people everywhere. He'd finally be able to transition away from this silly sport and into the sillier machinations of the underweb. The doctors gave his shoulders two more seasons but all the media experts said Web 4.0 was infinite.

###

The scary thing is I think Green is actually earnestly processing her grief in public like that's gonna help her feel anything.

Six may have a 6-figure salary and 6-figure followers but let's be serious,

I'm worried about Green's pretty visible loss in muscle mass

she did what, 3 obscure brand deals, 1 fashion week from a tired brand that shamelessly cast an influencer from every industry to try to go viral but nobody cared

Isn't it funny how Green's only decided to care about systemic violence when it affects people like her? And she has this platform because she just cares that much?

I feel like the crowds at each game are getting rowdier and rowdier.

And nobody outside of men's volleyball and sad trans people (hi) cares who she is

Yeah, totally, her eyes look eerily empty

Can you cis-people find anything else to get worked up over? There are wars happening. People are dying!

Do you think Green has an ED?

No, Green's definitely been vocal about police violence and abolition. Remember her tacky protest photos from last year?

It's also funny because Six just made that one post and dipped. Such complete opposites, I wonder if they talk about it at all.

ED like erectile dysfunction? She may be the most virile person I've ever met but she is trans so

Calling a woman virile is disgusting!

Plus Green's salary is like 70% deferred performance bonuses and stock options

If Green's team doesn't make it to the final, I feel like people might actually riot. You've got random bros betting thousands on Six and Green as a joke but the money is real.

And the rumors about Six's six-figure salary were started by her team so that

Maybe the revolution would be televised if it were a sport.

No, ED as in eating disorder!

Six and Green just give the media another reason to ignore the actual women's league.

The overlords are charging us to watch our own social death but maybe channel 999 forecasts the end of capitalism!

###

Without Green, Six wouldn't have known she was the breakout star of the tournament. Green was, of course, thrilled for her. She couldn't have reproduced Six's narrative anyway. Everyone took it for granted that Regalado would be in the finals because they took it for granted that Green was one of their stars. And once stars shone for long enough, their light was no longer newsworthy.

Conversely, Six's mid-career underdog-comeback primed critics and coaches to view her with both awe and nostalgia, a combination that made it easy for them to say things like, "These were the best performances of her career." It was primetime Sonus coverage.

Six had just helped Czwartek win their semifinal. After Aracaju took the third set, it looked like they might reverse Czwartek's momentum, but the fourth set was a wash. At the net, Curtis told her, I'm not mad, but I can't look at you right now. Henry said, Of course she did, and left it at that. She was in the stands with them now, not that Green could or wanted to make her out. Regalado was halfway through their semifinal match against the Ibaraki Jets, who'd made it out of Czwartek's pool second seed.

The last time she'd seen Thom and Eric was during last week's promo shoot. It felt like a year ago. Eric looked almost bored and Thom was dripping so much, he was making the floor sweepers sweat too. Sonus would be happy with either its golden boys or Green making the final. Ibaraki had won the first two sets easily; Regalado had just scraped wins in the second two. In this fifth and final set, Green could feel the chance to play Czwartek in the final slipping away. She didn't want to take the bronze medal from Aracaju. She wanted the climax to be her and Six. After the unprecedented confluence between recent tragedies, a gold medal rematch wasn't just a marketing opportunity but a political responsibility. She had to play it right—not just these silly ball games, but the real game of life.

Over the last week, she had scheduled extra sessions with Guthrie to help her unlock new nuances in her performances for the Fuck Your Exotic Fantasy panel and *Pacific* interview. She had done everything in her power to convince the world to treat Asian trans women like real people. And just as she had counted on Guthrie to help her sound solemn but confident, now she needed Griffin to at least pass the ball.

As Eric lined up his ball to serve, she couldn't think about whether engaging in critique could undermine the entire political project. She clapped her hands together. Hurtling to her team's side of the court at 122 kilometers an hour, the ball looked like it was going long but Griffin dove after it. He barely got the ball in the air but Green sprang to the side and squatted to get under it and set it to Luca, who spiked it. Ibaraki's new libero dug it and their bald setter passed it to Eric. Tracing his path, Green prepared to block alongside Ken. Together, they jumped and Green willed herself to lift higher and higher. She made her fingers iron upon contact. The ball bounced off her splayed hands and hit Ibaraki's side of the court.

Yes! she squealed, not turning away from Eric's face, finally conveying some emotion. The internet randos hadn't gotten to her but she'd gotten to him. Community in-fighting wasn't so different from volleyball. She couldn't take every lost point or mean comment personally. She had to narrow her focus on what really mattered: being better.

The big screen displayed MONSTER BLOCK and replayed the solidity of her wrists against Eric's swing. Green performed a rare but triumphant fist pump and flicked her ponytail around, reminding Thom and Eric and everyone watching in the stadium and all her haters online that she had the power to block too.

As her team huddled, she saw her reaction to her block playing on the big screen. She made a note to send "Being trans is my superpower" as a caption idea to Yemma. Ken gave her a particularly forceful thump on her shoulder blade. When the boys didn't treat her delicately, you knew they were pumped.

Regalado was still behind 10–13. They had to get to 15 and clear Ibaraki by 2 points.

Ken went to serve and Green zeroed back in. She couldn't get ahead of herself. She bent down and swayed her hips side to side. Ibaraki managed to skim his floater across the top of the net tape and the ball just plopped over to Regalado's side. Ricky lunged to catch it only for the ball to bump into the net and hit the floor anyway. In the back court, Griffin made a delayed, unenthused run to the front of the court. Useless. Thom eyed Green and smirked. She held her jaw strong. 10–14 Regalado. Match point Ibaraki.

Thom went back to serve. Green felt her team tense up. Thom sent the ball into the net. Green exhaled and smirked back. 11–14 Regalado.

It was Green up to serve. She swung her ponytail behind her back. From practices to games, she had served hundreds of times this tournament alone. Dribble, dribble. Spin the ball between her fingers. Dribble. Small toss. Eye the ball in her left hand. Big toss in the air, bound forward and jump. Hit with fingers wide.

It looked like it just grazed the line but the ref called it out. 15–11 Ibaraki. Before Ibaraki could celebrate, Oliver called a video review. As Regalado huddled during the wait, he babbled his platitudes about staying calm. Poor Will hopped up and down on the outside of the huddle, ever ready to take Griffin's spot even though he knew it wouldn't happen. Walt watched glumly from the bench.

Green felt a twinge of nervousness but shook it away. Service errors were fairly high especially at this highest level of sport, but she prided herself on her above-average accuracy.

While waiting for the refs to review the tape, she willed the ball to have been a precise ace from the league's shortest woman. It wasn't just a pivotal moment in her career—the very future of Asian trans women depended on the ref's call.

###

I thought Green meant on, not off . . .

The way Green sweat off her cakey makeup and you could see the lines around her eyes! Why is she giving such a bad name to Asian don't raisin?

We have to protect Green at all costs! We can't lose her too!

What if society didn't scam trans people into being so hypervigilant? Maybe they could just live!

What's Green's skin care routine because, um, I don't want that!

When they panned to Six and she looked so nervous, she really held that for all of us

I don't know if I can watch tomorrow's final, I might literally hurl my guts out

They just had to close up on Six during Green's game, they couldn't let Green have her own moment. Even on the court playing for another team, she has to be Six's girlfriend.

I can't believe nearly the entire tournament is over and there still aren't charges against the murderer or the cop who was on the scene.

Bestie would never do this but Green didn't credit @theLouisLens for shooting her

Is Green actually hot or can you just get a glimpse of that

sexy little clavicle when she drops her arms and her jersey dances around her neck?

*for shooting her in the Pacific! @theLouisLens

There were some sketchy calls today but nobody's talking about how important paying off the ref is

Who's the "we" Green? You and Six? You on behalf of all Asian femmes? Keep your pronouns to yourself

Relax @TeamSupaGreen pretty sure they called Six "Green's girlfriend"

###

Part corporate cafeteria, part faux-ski lodge, the hotel dining area felt more like summer camp as all these players and coaches tossed their gear and sweat everywhere. Six found a table in a corner and waited for Green.

Six, my star! Congrats on an incredible match today.

Six turned. Hi, Phil, thanks! she said. Her smile felt tense in her cheeks. Is this what Green felt when they were doing their show?

Really, you were just incredible. And that second semi—that was so close.

It really was.

But she did it. I mean, Regalado did it. And we get a rematch! What a treat. Phil beamed and slapped Six's bare shoulder as if they were volleybros. But he was just corporate Phil.

Hey, you! Wanna get food?

Now it was Henry who grabbed Six's shoulder. She reached around and put an arm around him and then Curtis.

I'll see you later, Phil, Six smiled. He acknowledged the boys and then was gone.

Why is he like that? Henry asked.

I know, so creepy, Curtis said. But really, he couldn't have asked for a better ratings outcome, right?

You would know, Six said. How many vlogs do you have left?

Curtis rolled his eyes as he spooned over-steamed broccoli onto his tray. I just have to film y'all tomorrow, edit ten hours of footage, and post three more.

Shout out to TriSpace for sponsoring these videos, Six quipped. But you haven't found a new editor yet?

No one up to the task. At least I'm saving some money?

So, Henry chimed in. Do you think you and your hefty shoulders are gonna be able to get it done again tomorrow? He slapped Six's shoulder again.

In the rape culture rule book, unfortunately Six wearing a tank top outside of work was asking for it.

Really, you were great! Curtis said as they reached their table.

Thanks—

I wasn't talking to you, I was talking to your gorgeous shoulders! Now Curtis smacked Six's bare shoulder.

Oh. Six laughed. With everybody touching my shoulders, they should get sponsored!

If your shoulder starts earning that athletic tape modeling money, just make sure to refer me. We'll do a video. Where's Green?

On her way—ahhh! Green! Baby puff!

Six spilled a cauliflower floret off one of her plates as she pushed through Henry and Curtis. She didn't mind the volley-bros who'd heard her yelp and had now turned to watch the league's sweethearts.

I'm so proud of you.

Thank you, Green said, a little blearily.

You did it. You played so well.

I know. I'm so relieved!

Congratulations! Curtis flapped his hands against Green's wrists with vigor. That was close.

When they reached 14, I honestly thought you were done for, Henry said. But then coming back for the win with that ace! That's my girl. Sorry, Six, but that's the semi they're going to remember!

And! Curtis said, you've been doing so many appearances and interviews this week. How've you been able to focus?

I'm feeling great! I'm so thankful for this beautiful life. Green's eyes did not look like they'd seen a five-set match just a few hours earlier.

Here, baby, eat up! Six slid a second tray her way.

But also, Curtis, you've actually been producing content. Now that's gotta be tough!

I know, Curtis said, but I'm mostly alone at my computer, whereas for you, it's like—

Like I'm being an attention whore? Green said, finding playful defensiveness with ease.

No, of course not! It's that you're having to respond to all this—Curtis twirled his wrist—in real time. I'll hit balls, but besides that, all they get are my hyperedited videos now.

She can't choose her destiny, Green said blithely. She can only embrace the path fate offers her.

And aren't we so proud of her? Henry said. Seriously, I didn't know I could admire you even more. Now he rubbed Green's slender, jacket-covered shoulder. Maybe it was just a touchy shoulder day all around.

Walt passed by with a plate of food. Hey, he said meekly, and seeing them all stare up at him, just stood there.

I'm Curtis! he beamed, his smile too big for the moment or the hour. He extended a hand.

I'm Walt. He slapped Curtis's hand, the sound like wet dough.

Henry introduced himself too.

What's up? Six asked.

Oh, just passing through. Walt shuffled, so plainly unsure. I—

SIX! From across the lounge, Alan came running up to them.

Six turned and waved.

Congrats again, Green, Walt said, and moped away.

What was that? Henry asked, trying not to laugh.

Oh, that's Walt, Green said. He's the other setter.

Alan! Six said.

Six! Alan's eyes shone as if he'd just cried or was about to cry again.

Alan! Six said again.

Six, I can't get over today. Alan pulled off his sweatshirt, as if still too hot from the excitement, and handed it wordlessly to Henry, who raised his eyebrows but draped it on a chair. Alan went on, his eyes gleaming, It was just incredible. I'm so happy for us. You got me into the Sonus final my first season.

What do you mean, Alan? We did it as a team.

Six pulled Alan in for a back-thumping hug. She felt like they'd had a version of this conversation on the court immediately after the game, and again in the locker room shortly after. You've been great, don't worry about it. Six's voice didn't deepen but it was bro-ier, her vowels wider, each sound booming from the breadth of her chest. It's what I would've hoped for in my first year as pro.

Exactly, Alan said. I'm so grateful to finally be playing with you. I don't know why Pete's waited all season.

Well, you know, Sam had earned his spot, Six began half-heartedly, and he—

Oh, shut up, you know it was bullshit. But you're a true class act, Six, the crème of the finest cream.

Henry's eyes bulged at this. Curtis covered his mouth.

Thanks, Alan. Do you know everyone?

After everyone said their names again, Alan reached forward to dap both Curtis and Henry, before asking Green, May I?

Uh, sure, Green said reflexively. Alan hugged her as if thanking her too. Perhaps he was.

Sorry, Green, but um, Alan began, your girlfriend and I are taking you down.

Huh. You think? Green cocked her head to the side.

Oh, definitely, Alan said, so earnestly it was more cute than threatening.

Okay then! Green beamed, her tone both emphatic and joking. Look at how she sustained the humorous moment. Even now, she was carrying herself as if a camera was recording her from all angles. She had to send Guthrie a gift when this was over.

Alrighty, I'm gonna inhale this and go to sleep. I'll see you tomorrow, Six! My favorite girl!

Alan! I'm like six years older than you!

Okay, fine, woman! Alan reached for another hug, holding on longer this time. Henry and Curtis continued staring, Henry's eyebrows raised, Curtis's mouth agape. Alan nearly skipped away with his tray.

Ooh, I was gonna say, Henry continued, as if they'd been gossiping the entire time, I wondered if Walt had a crush on you, Green. But since he's your sub, maybe he was just trying to curse you—

Guys! Green said.

—but Six, Henry went on, I *know* Alan has a crush on you.

Walt was now chatting with some other players but still looked so out of place. He was nodding too much.

So, Green, which do you think it is? Henry asked.

Don't be ridiculous, she laughed. A week ago, their Live chat about jealousy made her wonder. After this weekend, she was so self-possessed, she said things like, So, Six, are you gonna cry again?

Green! Why would you put me on the spot like this?

What do you mean? I just want to know what I'm getting myself into. Now Green slapped Six's shoulder playfully. It was totally okay when she did it.

Or you're trying to psych me out. Distract me from beating you.

Six! Green swatted at Six's shoulder again, this time squeezing it a little in her hand.

Hey!

Green turned. It was Thom. With Eric. Why did everyone want to talk to them?

Oh, hey! Six said.

Henry and Curtis stood and shook their hands.

Hey, Six! What's up, lady? Thom clapped Six on the back and Eric clapped her shoulder.

Green saw the greeting and was a little relieved and a little annoyed. She didn't want to not be touched when everyone seemed to be touching her girlfriend.

Congrats again, Green! Eric said. Good one today.

You really pulled that together at the last minute. We thought we had you. Thom winked.

Thanks, Green said, trying to not bare her teeth.

Really glad the world's gonna get to see you two make out on television again. Should be an exciting match! Thom went on.

I'm sure that'll be your favorite part, Curtis said.

If you want to hit on Green, you don't have to try so hard, Six said. She can reject you to your face if you want.

Six, relax, Green said.

Seriously, I really did appreciate y'all's video for *The Pacific*, Eric said.

Uh-huh, Six said. Good night.

The golden boy bros left and now the conversation could finally flow with cinematic sitcom ease of friends chit-chatting.

Curtis: They're so obsessed with you.

Six, waving her hand dismissively: Just brush these sad little dicks to the side and move on.

Henry, sitting back down: Why not just ignore them completely?

Green: Well, if we don't meet their digs, they'll think we're being snobby or bad sports or whatever.

Henry nodded, chewing meaningfully on a bite of pasta.

Six: Are you saying y'all don't have to deal with this?

Henry: Not really. Well, Curtis does a little more than me.

Curtis: But it's just like annoying jokes from this one guy on our team sometimes. It's not like random dudes from other teams go out of their way to make an ass out of us.

Green: But you'd respond the same way we just did, right?

Curtis: Yeah, I guess we would.

Green: Anyway, you boys played so well.

Henry: If only you weren't starting, Six, we definitely would've made the final.

Six: Aww, love you too, Henry!

The tall gay boys and tall gay girls all sat and ate with weary calm. Green eyed her face-down phone. Henry made a joke about the power of Green's hair to fend off jealous boys with male pattern baldness. She knew it was crass and even transphobic, but she realized she was actually too tired to banter anymore. Luckily Six was there.

Six: Ah yes, trans women are only powerful if we have long hair.

Green looked to the boys.

Henry: Yes, it's true, it's why my masculinity is so fragile. I'm just so repressed.

They all laughed at this slightly better joke. From one of their mouths, a speckle of spit flew into the air, totally free of viral matter.

Back in Six's room an hour later, Green could finally do it. On her girlfriend's bed, she swiped methodically. Thom and Eric had both gained followers, she noted in her mind, that private place where she didn't pretend she didn't track these things.

Six: I'm proud of you.

Six kissed Green on the cheek.

Green: Ehh, uhh, mm.

Green gave a quick peck on Six's lips.

Henry and Curtis had also gained more followers despite not making the final. Yesterday, they had posted and tagged Six and Green in the group promo they filmed last week.

Six: Green?

Green remembered that Sonus had shared the boy version of the group promo in more posts and stories than the gay version. She shook her head. What's up?

Six: Do you want to hang out with me?

Green hadn't reciprocated her congratulations, and so Six chose neediness. Even though they were together and alone, the rhythm of the conversation had gone. They had exited buddy sitcomland.

Green said, Sorry, I just want to make sure I'm up to date.

Not that there was conflict, just tension waiting to spill out.

With all the strangers interacting with you as if you're friends?

Green put her phone down. No. I mean, not just them. Did you hear about the latest bill proposal in Montana?

Not yet?

Well apparently, they just brought it to the floor today and everyone's posting about it.

Oh. Are people organizing against it? Six shuffled awkwardly. Maybe that was the wrong question.

Green turned her face away from her phone to look at her girlfriend. Six. C'mon.

What?

This is important. Like these kids' lives are going to be fucked if we don't do something. Obviously people are organizing.

Six would not acknowledge Green's impatience, not directly. She didn't want to get into it. Not tonight. I'm not saying it's not important. You know I'm so proud of you for using your platform to speak up. I just hope you're not feeling like you have to say something just because everyone else is. Of course I'm worried and I'm scared but I have no idea what the bill is about and I don't know if looking it up would help me or help them right now.

Well, this is happening now, Green said, sitting up. Like,

do you know how privileged we are to do what we're doing right now?

Seriously, Green? Of course I do. I'm just—

This is happening now! Green said again, patting the mattress with urgency this time. If we just wait, it'll just happen, and then we'll be wishing we had done something sooner.

You're not wrong.

But I'm not right either? Green clutched her phone like it was charging her.

You know, I'm not going to try to tell you what to do. I support you. If you don't feel like hanging out, I'm gonna go to sleep. We can do this after tomorrow's match.

Six, c'mon.

What, Green? Six sat up too, crossing her arms in a defiantly womanish way.

It wasn't funny because it was womanish. It was funny because it was Six.

Six, I love you.

I love you too, Green.

Just give me a few minutes.

Six rolled her eyes dramatically. As she scooched back against the headboard, one of her legs flopped atop Green's.

Ugh, I'll hurry! Green rubbed Six's ankle with one hand as she continued scrolling evenly on her little phone.

Six rolled over. I'm gonna shower.

Mmm, Green said.

While the water ran, Green began typing: "This is an outrage! One horror after another." She was emotional but her thumbs wrote with cold purpose. She encouraged people to make those phone calls, to make donations to those organizers, to talk to those neighbors. She finally understood the power of her voice. Here was another tragedy affecting everyone but not swaying enough people in the right direction. It was exhausting, though. Six was probably right. But she refused to settle for that sort of fatalism. She proofread her post.

Six emerged from the bathroom, her hair in a floppy bun, her body still dripping wet. She was drying herself off absently with a towel too tiny for such a tall person. Her shower had only slightly dulled her irritation.

Green gave an emphatic tap and finally set her phone face down. She looked up at her nearly naked girlfriend.

Hi, Sixy, Green said.

Six looked at Green looking at her. Seriously? Six asked, laughing. Being in the same room with Green saying her name this attentively for the first time in months almost made it sound new.

Green had done her job for trans people. Now she had to be a good girlfriend. She reached toward Six and tugged at her towel-free hand. Six plopped onto the bed.

Hi, Green said again. She knew what counted.

Lying on her stomach, Six softened. She knew Green knew what she was doing. But it wasn't wrong. Not tonight, at least. Trying to talk about it would only make her annoyed again.

This past week has put such a strain on us both, Green began.

Yeah, she said.

I'm just glad we're here for each other. Thank you for supporting me.

It was a little mechanical, but it would do. At least Green could rub her shoulder in a way no one could. Six scooched forward, arching her back to wrap her arms around Green's waist. Same here, baby. She squeezed the flesh beneath Green's ribs.

Six! Are you really holding on to me like this? Green's voice sparkled, lightening the mood another gradient.

Yes, dear, she replied into Green's thighs.

Green brought her hands to Six's scalp and she felt Six weaken when she caressed her neck.

It did matter that there was a big game tomorrow. If they could make nice, Six would sleep better, which would make her feel more focused and agile for the game. She'd have a nimbleness that was hard to conjure in warm-up alone. They hadn't been the kind of athletes who liked to have sex before a big game, but maybe the pandemic had made them a couple who wanted to have sex in those rare moments they could, together, in-person.

Six pressed her head into Green's stomach and Green leaned back against the headboard. Six reached up Green's T-shirt till she found her shoulders and pulled like they were a bar at the gym. Green kissed Six's temple and felt Six sink into her even more. She leaned back to scoop Six up from below her ribs, her hands grazing her butt and lower back. Six's towel got caught between their legs as she brought her face level to Green's. Her face looked so weary. She was so beautiful this way. Six smiled at Green's softened expression. Was Green tearing up? She threw her arms around Green's neck and pressed her lips into Green's already parted mouth.

Thank goodness they'd stopped trying to talk about anything.

Green traced the plump outline of Six's bottom lip, pressing the familiar shape and density between her own. It tasted so good. She breathed. She bit. Six whimpered softly. Green's arms hooked beneath Six's armpit and she squeezed those gorgeous, gorgeous shoulders to her.

Six brought her hands from Green's neck to her waist and kissed her more. I'm going to take your T-shirt off, she said.

Please, Green said.

Six's hands tugged the soft cotton off before she kissed Green's neck, moving down to her sternum. Green loved Six's body. It moved so wondrously in response to hers. It reminded her why she cared so much.

Six reached for the waistband of Green's sweatpants. Green slithered her pelvis and legs against Six as she helped Six undress her, finally. Six loved how Green let her core disengage just a bit so her flesh gave in to her touch. All she had wanted was to feel that her girlfriend was present with her. You smell so good, she whispered. She gulped Green's scent, the same as ever. It transformed Six's exasperation into compassion. Green breathed more heavily now too. They couldn't be closer but still, they pressed and pulled.

And even though the end of the tournament meant they'd soon share a summer layoff, tonight felt precious. After all the ways they'd been documented and observed over the last week, so intimately and yet impersonally, they finally got to just hold each other.

It wasn't late but it wasn't early and even if they weren't

thinking about it, they both knew where they had to be the next day. They both knew they'd have to sleep and couldn't just lose themselves in the ravishing sensation of each other's bodies. Not tonight.

And so, with some urgency, they touched, kissed, inhaled every part of each other with every part of each other that they could reach. When they were done, it wasn't over.

###

Green's ass looks even more incredible than I thought it would, fuck

Omg where did this come from?

YUMMY!

Is that my Green? My sweet precious Greenie?

Guys, this is clearly a deepfake, a perverted, super sexy deepfake

If there's one, that means there are more of these right? How do we get them to drop more?

Guys, she's wearing a strap on! I knew it! Attagirl!

Fuck, I just pounded one out but I'm already hard again

Nope @brownbuttercarrotcake pretty sure that's Green's ass, I ate her out for 3 hours at a party once

We knew Six was baby girl but a BOTTOM?!

Great two people who look like sexless toy dolls made a porno how original

I feel like I shouldn't be watching this but, what am I gonna do? Not watch it?

Damn Six, now I see what you see in her

If anyone was in doubt about Six's womanhood, what do you have to say to this? Huh?

Are we sure this isn't @sixpointfive & @spearmintgreen?

Where did Six get that backless teddy? God she looks so good in lace

I'm so happy that they have such passionate sex

This video dropping today of all days . . .

Wow this should be in the textbook for hatefucking

Stop watching you perverts!!

Make sure to save a copy to the spank bank before it gets deleted!

Baby trans girls having sex is so embarrassing. I wish they'd just chop it off already

Maybe I want an LDR too! If you miss your boo that much and the sex is this good.

It almost feels like it's the early 2000s again, remember every month was another celebrity sex tape?

Those cheeks!! Who knew Green had that in her? A voracious little rabbit, isn't she!

Isn't it ironic how Japan colonized Vietnam and now Green colonized Six's pussy?

My kid thinks he's trans. I'm gonna show him this is what happens if he tries to be a sissy like Six and Green

It makes sense actually. Green is pretty uptight in public, so no surprise she's like this in bed

That's not irony, that's reification!

Do you think Green did this on her own or did her agent orchestrate this or is her agent furiously calling her now, asking her wtf she was thinking?

Guys what if it was Six who leaked it?

I want someone to cup my tits the way Green cups Six's tits

Why would Six leak it? What would she want out of this? To tell the world she's open for business when she loses tomorrow?

This was obviously staged, when else do two people cum at the same time on camera?

Six has such a pretty pussy

The final is later today? I will never again complain about the universe ghosting me.

Use my code SPIKECITY for 5% off your first month of Sonus Premium!

Is Green a . . . service top?

It's very sweet how they're engaging in the reproductive act of sex after last week's murders. It's so life affirming to watch them choose hope

@theory4babes you know they can't actually get pregnant right? Like that's not how that works?

Six holding on to Green for dear life is such a mood

Omg Six why are you spanking Green like that??

@tim3290 this is actually an old video, Six doesn't have her tricep tattoo

@treeofeve sex isn't always about making babies, stop being so literal and grow a heart, you fucking rationalist

That was hot but it won't supplant that slomo of Six squeezing Kenny's waist beneath his jersey. DM if u haven't seen it.

Did you not hear Green telling her to smack it harder?

@treeofeve if you want me to shove something down your fucking pervert throat just send me a goddamn fucking DM

We knew Six was a brat on live but this is next level

And look at Green getting off on it, who knew she was so kinky

Sonus is about to make so much money

Guys, this is not KINK. Some of you have only had vanilla sex like Six and Green and it SHOWS

Can someone confirm the audio? Did Green say "tell me what makes you happy baby girl?"

@spikycity if you wanna watch two girl dudes fuck that's okay too, you don't have to convince anyone here, we're all telling on ourselves. Wanna unlearn our shame together? Haha

###

Everybody complained about that site's glitches and poor video quality but they all still used it anyway. It had worked for him. Given the pandemic's inspiration of new pornographic interests, this video would titillate even more eyeballs. They would all see that shameful secret and make it a shared joke. The sex positivity and corrupted gender equality movement had made people think anyone having sex was hot, even two transtrenders. But it hadn't gone so far as to stop people making fun of other people fucking.

He (@transaretrans, 112k followers) sat atop his hotel comforter. He cracked his neck and drafted the post on his growing educational account. First, he chose a screenshot from the video with the PornTub watermark. Next, he took a couple emojis of the woman with the pale face and dark black hair shrugging and placed them tastefully over Six's and Green's genitalia. Finally, he wrote the caption, compiling all the stray threads that had slow-cooked in his head all week. Each sentence unfurled crisp and exacting. Time was a healer of all wounds, a buffer against all surfaces. He reviewed it one last time, top to bottom, and scheduled it to go live in one hour.

It'd been too easy. Six's phone had spread open at his touch, still unlocked, the explicit videos saved in a folder labeled *sweet loving*. He'd discreetly AirLifted them to himself and returned it to Six. He assessed the files' varying eroticisms with an almost clinical distance. But he hadn't yet watched the winner.

Now, he could finally watch the original file and take it in, let himself grow hot at the collar. He still didn't hate Six like he hated Green but two weeks in this bubble with them had made them both insufferable. He hit *play*. Seeing them touch each other, his armpits grew clammy. Between his legs, his penis flapped at his thighs before pushing against his pajama pants. He pulled his dick from the elastic waistband of his shorts and reached for the hotel sample lotion and squirted some out. Fuck, he said as Green tore Six's blouse off. They were terrible people but so hot. He had spent his whole adolescence erasing any trace of effeminacy. Then he'd become gay and been erased for being Asian. And now his trailblazing career as an Asian man was being ignored because two trans Asian girls were doing it better. He was supposed to be the first but he'd been so close to them, he could've only been eclipsed by their fame seeking. They had done it well. He wanted so badly to tear off Six's tank top earlier that evening in the lounge.

He'd been so close to her tremendously elegant muscles. But it wasn't Six he was ogling now.

He turned up the volume on his computer just as Six bit her lip and moaned. He noticed the way the moody lighting struck Green's jaw, long and straight but not hard, not at all like a man's jaw. As they kissed each other, loudly, he encircled his dick and began stroking, the excess lotion nearly slipping off onto the bed. He turned the computer around and went to the bathroom where he grabbed a spare towel.

Six had Green pressed up against a window now. As Six kissed Green's neck ferociously, he pictured himself in Green's place but also being the one pushing Green against a window. He then pictured himself grabbing Green's pussy the way Six was now. He slitted his eyes and saw himself tearing away Green's underwear. He then had to picture himself turning Green around because it was actually Six being turned around in the video. It felt so good in his mind. He grunted, for no one. As Six, or Green in his imagination, arched her sinewy, supple back for him, before Green could even enter him, Henry came between his hands, spurting his three droplets onto the towel before the video was even a quarter of the way through.

###

Green was so stunned, she couldn't feel horrified. Yemma, she said. Are you ser—Yemma, this isn't funny.

Yemma cried too. Green was still confused but tears streamed down her already puffy morning face, which she hadn't even washed or jade-rolled or serumed yet. Green was back in Six's room. She'd fled her room when Yemma called, thankfully not crossing anyone in the hallways or elevators on her way down.

I know, sweetie, Brent said on speaker. We had it taken down and have blocked any variations of it from being posted again. But it was out there for a good forty-five minutes before—

Right, okay, Green said.

Six hadn't said a word. She was lying on her bed, her phone between her and Green, who was seated with her back to Six.

So what do we do now? Green asked.

I've spoken with the league, Yemma said. Thankfully they've agreed to take you out of media obligations this morning. You don't have to say anything before the game. But just do your best to just play. Do this part of your job and try to—

But how? How am I supposed to play fucking volleyball when I don't know how many thousands of strangers have seen some video of me and Six having sex on their phones? Can't they postpone the game?

Brent and Yemma were in a three-way audio call with the girls; in a separate muted video call, Yemma made a knowing look to Brent, who nodded in return, agreeing that they did not yet have to tell her that in fact, the two-minute clip had received over three million views on PornTub before being removed.

Green, Six, Yemma began. We are so sorry this happened to you. It's so unfair. So pathetic.

It's racist! Green shouted at the phone. It's transphobic! It's a fucking hate crime!

I know, sweetie, Brent said.

Don't fucking "sweetie" me, Brent, Green said. It's not your sex tape floating around for all the fucking perverts to get off to.

Six cried silently.

You're right, Brent said.

None of you know! None of you! Green said. People don't fetishize you like they do us.

Green, Six said softly through her tears.

Yemma said, It's true. We can't even imagine.

Of course not, Brent said.

Green, Six said again. Greenie.

What? Are you trying to tell me to calm down? Green snapped, not turning around.

Six reached for Green's hand. Green, she said again, louder, her voice breaking. I'm not. Please. I'm here for you. Please. She found Green's wrist, dry and unlotioned, and squeezed. She wished Green would squeeze hers back.

I can't believe this is happening! Green sobbed. She let Six pull her into her arms. She heard Six's quiet sniffles through her own louder wailing. Six's tears fell into Green's morning hair, tangled and lank.

We are so sorry, Brent said again. On their side call, Yemma nodded for him to go on. We wish we could've stopped this sooner, we wish we could've prevented this from happening at all.

Green bawled between Six's arms. She couldn't speak.

Six stayed quiet, crying for herself, for her girlfriend,

for their privacy, stolen so easily. They'd filmed some videos during last summer's layoff when they found out the league would be resuming an approximate version of its normal schedule. The pandemic-era honeymoon they'd so quickly taken for granted had come to an abrupt end. They just wanted to remember it.

Try and let yourself cry, Yemma said. At least while you can. Stay offline. But we can't postpone the game. We tried but it's in your contract with the league. This doesn't fall under force majeure, so you can't sub out. All the other players, the arena, the staff are counting on today.

This time, it was Brent who gave the supportive nod. They both had more difficult clients but had learned over the last year how delicate this team was.

Yemma went on, When it's time, I know you can do what you have to do. You've got to. Put on your game faces, put on your camera faces. Warm up. Stretch. Find your connection with your teammates. And play some awe-inspiring volleyball. Okay? Don't let whoever did this take this day from you. Because you know that's exactly why they chose today. Don't let them win.

Six heard how Yemma tactfully buried the word *contract* in the middle of her pep talk, skillfully eliding the heart of it all—the money, the losses they could afford, the ones they wouldn't stand for, Yemma and Brent's commission. Thanks, Yemma, she said, her voice only wavering slightly. Is there anything else we should know?

Just, Brent began. Just try to redirect this into the ball. Not at each other, but you know, play good.

Thanks, Brent. We'll talk later?

Of course. Love you, Six. Love you, Green.

Love you!

Green was now wordless. Six tried to feel comfort in the weight of Green's body, even if she craved some reciprocal force too. But unlike the last month, she didn't mind its absence. Not right now. I wish I could say anything useful, she said into Green's scalp. Caretaking came so naturally to her. She murmured, We have to do this for us. It's not just a contract but a career that we love. We can be hurt but we can't hide. Not yet. We're gonna get through this, baby.

Green nodded against Six's chest. The sex they'd had last night wasn't even a memory. Green couldn't fathom anything before waking up to that news. There was only this never-ending moment she'd never able to return from.

But the clock kept ticking. They had to leave the hotel in thirty minutes. They'd have to de-puff Green's eyes and put on their faces. They had to eat. Six guessed Green wouldn't want to but they had to. Maybe they could skip their personal warm-up and let their muscles convulse until they had to play. All they had were meaningless minor choices over their bodies. Since the murders, they had forgotten how big the game was.

###

So they're still on? he asked.

Brent sighed. Yeah, they'll be there.

Phil mirrored Brent's sigh. To show compassion. He said, Well, they are champions.

Yeah, Yemma said, they are.

Well, I really appreciate you both, I can't imagine what you must feel. Phil's sympathetic tone was jovial despite the subject of the call.

No problem, Brent said.

I have to go deal with this but keep me posted.

Of course, you do the same, Yemma said.

Yemma, Brent, and Phil all hung up.

Yemma dialed lawyers, bypassing their administrative assistants.

Brent sent the email he'd been writing on the call. He wished he had flown out for the tournament. He could've at least been there.

Phil looked out his hotel window. He was staying on the top floor above all the players. He loved the new arena but thankfully did not live in this little shithole of a resort town year-round. He could not have expected this.

Brent picked up a call from his partner. No, he couldn't get the kids, major work crisis, but like, seriously this time. He heard a sigh and a click.

Phil called his assistant and the sweetheart picked up his phone on the second ring. He loved having someone on call.

###

There. He'd done what he needed to. He had to see the video. It was his job, after all. He downloaded it and reached into his boxers.

###

Walt hadn't been awake while the original video circulated but everyone was talking about it so it wasn't hard to find. Not these days. As TV networks and musicians became more aggressive about censoring unlicensed reproductions of their intellectual property, content consumers became more adept at blasting ripped files through every firewall corporations could code. So when she'd rolled over into the morning sun glaring between the curtains and checked the forums, she just had to comb through 287 posts in the last five hours, dozens more already deleted. She'd gathered from the replies that some members had not only posted the original link but links to its repostings since its deletion. They had all been chastised but half had disappeared to other forums where they wouldn't and couldn't apologize to the people who cared.

Walt's curiosity was louder than her shame. She wasn't watching to masturbate. She watched to be in the know. She had to understand all the references people had made and would continue to make. But she also wanted to learn what kind of women Green and Six were with each other. She watched to learn what kind of woman she herself might be.

She hit *play*. She was momentarily aroused and then felt guilty for being aroused by her teammate's violation of privacy. She felt dread. She didn't want this, not for herself, not for Green or Six. How could she ever become a girl if this was what happened to girls like her? Or at least, to girls as stunning as they were. She caught her own image in the mirror and groaned. Dysphoria was forever.

Then, she wondered if Green would be up to playing today. She checked her email and saw no updates from Oliver.

The team group chat was also empty—unusual for a game day. Someone should have sent a *Good morning!* by now. Or at least some fire emojis.

Walt returned to the video and watched it to the end, fascinated and disgusted. She was surprised by the quality of Green's forceful physicality. And the quality of her musculature. She had never seen Green topless and now appreciated how a square jersey smothered a body worthy of poetry. And Six—her charisma never failed to translate. The third viewing, she felt weirdly happy for them. At least they seemed to have nice sex. Maybe she might have nice sex with someone someday. If Green could thrust her hips like that, maybe Walt could too. She already felt kinda sick. She stopped pretending it'd just be one more viewing and made the clip full screen.

###

B314? Right this way!

Totally, Czwartek's played really well this tournament.

I WANT IT ALL! I WANT IT NOW!

Sorry, you're in my seat.

What?

Yeah, revenge porn is so predictable.

B314! See? Would you mind?

I wonder who's gonna get fired for not prepping them.

Just so you know, we're asking all guests to try to keep their masks on when not eating or drinking, all right?

Six and Green! Six and Green! Six and Green!

I bet Regalado takes it, let's say, in four sets.

Oh, P314. What do you mean I'm all the way up there?

It sucks what happened to her. But she chose to be famous, you know?

Wait, what video are you talking about?

But what about them? They're not eating and they don't have a mask!

As you can see, we have an already electric crowd here at the second annual Sonus Volleyball Tournament. Tonight's the gold medal match between Czwartek and Regalado, the two top-seeded teams, and they've both played spectacularly this tournament.

This sick sex tape of Six and Green, when I first watched it, I moaned like you wouldn't believe!

Rudy Barnes here with two-time World Cup MVP Tanner Hughes. Tanner, what can we expect for today's match?

And then I groaned.

Wait, Green's not playing?

I heard Six punched a reporter in the lobby.

Wait, which one is Six and which one's Green?

Mhm, Green withdrew from the tournament this morning.

What?? Are you serious?

Well, the volleyball world has shuffled around a lot these past couple seasons.

Someone else was saying Six got disqualified for unsportswomanlike behavior.

That's so cruel. We didn't take a fifteen-hour flight to not see them play against each other.

No. NO! Green would NEVER withdraw, trust me,

nobody knows her like ME. I've seen every episode of *Six & Green* five times.

Wooooooo!

There are ten major leagues across the world, each with their own tournaments.

No, I totally get it. Here's my cheat sheet.

So Six is actually sidelined and Green withdrew because she was so embarrassed that her girlfriend can't control her temper.

WOOOOO!!!

Sonus has been growing volleyball over the last decade and created this tournament to crown the best club team in the world.

No, it's not a race or a gender thing, it's that all celebrities look the same.

We need BIPOC trans commentators!

Six! Six! Six! Six!

You know we have to ask for a white cis woman commentator first. Then a BIPOC cis man. Left foot, right foot!

National teams only play together a couple months a year but with club teams, players build that team chemistry over an entire season, so tonight you're going to see the fastest balls you'll see all year.

Did you see Six graze Alan's ass? What a pervert, I can't believe he has to put up with that.

As you can see while Czwartek makes their entrance, we're playing in a brand-new, state-of-the-art arena. Isn't she a beauty?

Oh em gee, he touched me! He touched me! I love you, Dan!

I wish something like the Sonus Tournament existed when I was playing.

Did you see Alan touch Six's ass? I hope she's okay.

Tanner, how does this kind of energy affect you as a player? Volleyball is huge in most of these teams' home countries, so they're used to enthusiasm. But this is something else, right?

Of course, she's okay with it. I bet they're fucking. Do you think Green knows?

Well, Rudy, it depends. When there's this much noise and you're under the bright lights, naturally your heart rate will tend to quicken.

I heard Six and Green broke up this morning after the video dropped.

I remember Green gave me an autograph when she was still playing at Lancaster. She shook my hand and told me I had talent. I just know that moment meant something to her.

Six found out that Green leaked the video and ended it.

For some players, they might get nervous and have to work harder to focus or rein in the adrenaline.

I just think the volleyball bubble is gonna burst if this game doesn't go well.

So Green didn't withdraw?

Would you sit your skinny ass down? I can't see!

For me, it didn't matter if I was jet-lagged or sore, a crowd always made me come alive.

How are Green's legs so skinny but she's so strong? Like what's she made out of?

Not my man Charlie. See Number 6 with the thick legs?

Why are there so many strobe lights? Does this turn into a club later?

Aww, it's sweet how they shake hands before shoving their balls in each other's faces.

Oh wow, okay. Is Charlie straight?

Size and strength don't necessarily correlate.

Did you see Green just rail Six in that tape?

Share pictures or videos of your Sonus Volleyball experience with the official hashtag #SVT2021.

Let's get loose, boys! And Green!

Should we go after Green? Now that we know she doesn't like to receive?

Yeah, Igor, go after Six's girlfriend. Sorry Six.

They only get five minutes to warm up? Broadcast schedules are endangering our athletes!

Czwartek! Czwartek! Czwartek!

As you can see, there are lots of eyes on all balls at all times:

Those horny comments had me laughing so hard I finally wept for the first time since the murders.

But they've never played a game this big after suffering so much tragedy so soon.

Nah, they've been here hours already, they're just doing a quick touch on the court beneath the arena lights.

Would you look at Six and Green's gym shorts? Why are they shorter than everyone else's?

Our team of refs watch for ball play, net violations, and call each point.

Let's get rowdy, Regalado!

So you have the tape? Can I see?

If you had their legs, you would wear shorter shorts too.

Sonus also has set up an extensive set of cameras for video reviews.

Dude relax, we can literally picture her naked now.

No, I mean look at Charlie's shorts. And Alan's. It's all the same short. Six and Green just have long legs.

Each team can request two per set. Any successful review does not count against those two, but once you have two failed challenges, the ref's call is final.

Why do they all look so tiny? Except for that one, Number 6 on Czwartek, do you see him?

Is Green playing or not? Is this just for show?

Leading up to his final match, Team Czwartek has a 5–0 record, winning their semi-final match yesterday against Aracaju in straight sets.

Number 6 is Six. Dude, did you see their jump serve? And their calves? Aren't they such a beast?

I finally get why Czwartek benched Six all year, she would've dogwalked all the other teams and the antitrust lawsuit against their dominance would've been a waste of everyone's time.

Regalado is coming in at 4–1 this tournament. Yesterday, they beat third-ranked Ibaraki in five sets in the longest match of this tournament thus far.

Six's pronouns are she/her!

So if I tackled Six, do you think he'd squeeze my neck between his juicy adductors to stop me from getting the ball?

This game has gotten a lot faster.

Some basketball players' legs are pretty skinny too. They just aren't wearing short shorts any more.

This isn't American football, there's no tackling.

Instead of the ball floating in the air for seconds at a time, when they're in system, you can hardly see where the ball is going.

Just intense eye contact and brushing your fingers against your rival's at the block.

Wait why is Czwartek's coach so short? I know people lose some height when they age but c'mon, that's just funny.

So volleyball players wear shorter shorts because they use their legs more?

And now for a special message from two of tonight's stars.

Dude, that's Petr Wozniak, one of the all-time greats. He's fifty-nine and still in incredible shape. He played in the seventies when the average male volleyball player was only 5 foot 8 inches.

Bro, don't get twisted by the teleology. If Six wants to get that floaty jump, she's gonna keep her legs trim and her shorts short.

I'm Six. I'm a middle blocker for Czwartek.

Wait, if he's only fifty-nine, how did he play in the seventies? That doesn't add up!

I'm Green. I'm the setter for Regalado.

It totally does, you're just bad at math.

We're both devastated by the recent news of three murdered trans women in Alpharetta.

You used to be able to fuck a tranny and kill her if she

got mouthy. And nobody cared! Now I have to sit and applaud these brawny pretenders?

It's endemic of ongoing violence against trans people in this country.

Now you get these transvestites rich and famous enough to afford private security, so that when they die, it's a national tragedy. America is a dying empire.

From horrific attacks like this one to the onslaught of anti-trans legislation proposed this year,

Doesn't Six play in Russia though? Don't they hate gay people over there?

Sonus Volley supports trans athletes and condemns these murders and any legislation that seeks to erase trans people living our lives to the fullest.

Six plays in Poland, not Russia. She's hardly said anything about living in Poland though.

We're not taking a sideline.

I can't believe we're watching Six and Green on a big screen and they're also, like, in the same room as us right now.

We're putting ourselves at the center.

So is Green playing or is she just here for show?

Sonus Sports and Sonus Volley have given us such a safe place to be our authentic selves.

Three girls are dead but now there's a new sex tape, it's old news. TO BEA! TO CLARISSE! TO SUZY!

As trans women, we can do our job without worrying about harassment.

Do you think Six is going to cry again?

We hope all trans women can find the same safety and support.

Playing that video again after that sex tape broke the internet is so uncanny. It's almost like, predictive technology.

We need to keep asking big questions about gender and race in our sport.

Do you mean like . . . ? Like they leaked it on purpose?

In the meantime,

Yeah. I think so.

We'll see you on the court!

Czwartek and Regalado last played each other in February, and Regalado won the match in four sets. At last year's inaugural tournament, Regalado won their semifinal in five.

They're both standing like they're always posing for some camera. As if anyone cares.

So even though Regalado has won three of their last four matchups, I gotta say, in terms of momentum, I gotta give a slight edge to Czwartek this tournament.

I doubt it. Six looked pretty stone-faced when she was walking down the aisle earlier. And Green looked like she was covering her face from the bright lights but honestly, she was covering her face from being seen, don't ya think?

Oh my god, are you crying? You realize this is still warm-up right?

Green's looking pretty focused, considering! God, she's so strong, this must be so tough for her.

It should be Ibaraki here, the ref yesterday was so biased in favor of Regalado.

Green just arched her back to let us know she likes to take it too.

Maybe Green dropped the tape to throw Six off her game?

They just mean so much to me!

I'd rather be watching Thom and Eric instead of these faggots.

Oh babe!

Six and Green have the worst fandom.

I heard Thom and Eric are fucking.

How long are they going to warm up for? START THE GAME!

Dude, what the fuck, just because you want them to fuck doesn't mean they're fucking.

And now, your starting lineups for the gold medal match of the 2021 Sonus Volleyball Tournament!

They're just bros being dudes. Stop making everything gay.

Yeah, no, they're definitely fucking. One of my friends delivered pizza to Eric and Thom opened the door with a towel on and he could see Eric naked in a mirror hanging on the wall.

First up, our top seed, Czwartek!

What hotel are the athletes staying at?

How many times a day do you think they high five each other?

Didn't you see that Seddit thread about all the boys Eric gave chlamydia to?

Number 7 is Czwartek's setter and team captain. He's been with Czwartek for fourteen years and still has the fastest serve on the team. It's Dan Humphries!

Green looks like she could kill someone.

It's so sad how they've bullied Eric into acting straight to maintain his reputation.

Why is Six already sweating so much, is she sick?

Next up, Number 3, opposite Igor Zielinski! He's played with Czwartek for eight seasons and stands 6 feet 9 inches.

I feel like that's not her glowing skin, I feel like she's already wet.

LET'S FUCKING GO!

Does Six have a fever? Is it the virus?

How do you know you're straight if you've never cupped your homie's cheeks and taste tested his dick?

Dude, you spilled your sauce all over me!

Number 4 is outside hitter Alan Baker! This is his first season with Czwartek and first as a pro. Welcome to big-time volleyball and your first Sonus Tournament.

Why did you wear a white shirt to a sports game?

Did Six not get sex last night? Is she so horny she's sweating?

What do you mean? The tournament sold out the day tickets went on sale.

It's no surprise she's Number 6. You just saw her on the big screen. It's middle blocker Six! She's played pro volleyball for eight years but just joined Czwartek this season. She stands 6 feet 7 inches tall and weighs 204 pounds.

Why are you looking at Six's Instagraph profile? She's right there!

Why did they just share Six's weight? Did they do that for the other players?

She really doesn't look too hot.

No, they said one of the boy's heights but not everyone's.

Number 9, Czwartek's other middle blocker James Akbari! This is his fifth season in the league. James likes to snowboard in the offseason.

Why did you drag me to a volleyball game?

Number 11, the libero! Emir Tabak! Emir is Czwartek's shortest player but wait till you see him dive across the floor. Hardly anyone faster!

Girl, what do you mean? You literally woke up at 4 a.m. for the pre-sale!

If only more kids left their bodies alone like Six and Green, instead of shooting themselves up with hormones.

Well, I just broke up with my boyfriend last week, you should've known this environment would be triggering.

Last but not least, Number 18! Outside hitter Kenny Kutza! This is his tenth and last season with Czwartek, so wish him a memorable last game.

I'm sorry, are you joking? I'm sorry about your sidepiece, but now your gaslighting is triggering ME!

Aww, so cute. Look at them with their arms around each other.

I don't want sports to be beautiful, I want the balls to fly fast everywhere.

Who?

Now on to Regalado! Not Kenny but Number 2! Team captain and outside Ken Cardoso! He's played for Regalado nine years and leads a mean HIIT warm-up.

Six and Alan.

The way that they arch their backs to spike the ball and land just before the midline.

Do you think they're fucking?

Number 4 is middle blocker Luca Bianchi. This is his sixteenth season with Regalado but he says he still has at least five more seasons left in him.

They're constantly improvising with such precision. It's like an interpretive dance.

Is that why Green dropped a sex tape? Like marking her territory?

Number 6 is middle blocker Charlie Auclair. He used to play opposite till he was recruited by Regalado right out of college six years ago. This season, he leads the overall rankings in blocks.

The way Luca is always fidgeting with his shirt hem is so slutty.

Alan is like, seven years younger than Six. Do you think that baby face has seen much?

So they're not allowed to cross the midline? It's like forbidden territory? That's so hot.

Number 9 is outside Ricky Gomez!

So what? It's not like he's a minor.

You're so gross.

Ricky outgrew the ceilings of his childhood home at age sixteen and when he turned pro, he moved into a penthouse and has never looked back.

Would it be gross if I lusted after Kenny or Ken or whoever?

Nope, not unless the ball hits the floor first. Basketball only has one place the ball can go to get a point but with volleyball, there are so many permutations.

Ricky, tell me you only date people under 5 foot 6! Please!

At 6 feet 11 inches, he's the tallest player starting on the court today.

No, because men should be objectified at all times.

That's a double standard! That's reverse sexism!

Number 14 is opposite spiker Bill Adler! This is Bill's third season with Regalado. When he's not on the court, he's a home baker and aspiring food photographer. He makes a gooey peach cobbler.

What hotel are the athletes staying at?

Okay, if you're seriously trying to question me on that here, you can just leave!

I can't tell if everyone's just pumped or if there's a weird energy in the air.

They arrested the murderer, right?

Number 19 is Green! A setter, she's been Regalado's playmaker for six seasons. She cares about advocating for trans athletes in pro sports.

Like bloodthirsty?

No, I'm not saying men should be objectified sexually, they should be objectified like literal objects.

Are you just that horny?

Yeah, he's in jail right now. I hope they give him hell?

And last but not least, your libero! Number 13, Will Fassen! Will's been a crucial Regalado member since 2016 and is stoked to be starting his second match of the season.

Yeah, I hear what you're saying but you still sound horny.

Apparently the murderer's still on the loose. What if he kills more innocent women?

You can't tell now, but just wait till they start playing!

You mean trans women?

They have the most spectacular, perky tits!

I was trying to include all women! You're not supposed to say "cis women and trans women" because—

Six dropped the sex tape to distract from her teammate getting accused of rape today, now that's a team player.

You detracted from his main targets, which were trans women, not cis women.

I've never heard of Six or Green before this week but I watched all the episodes of their show last night. Does that happen to everyone?

I heard Green doesn't but Six does. They were both going to get bottom surgery in Thailand but then Six chickened out at the last minute.

GREEN, I WOULD NEVER LET ANYONE TOUCH YOU BUT ME!

From her balls, duh!

Wait, what happened to Griffin?! I just noticed he's not on the court.

God, you ask people to quarantine for not even a year and everyone's rabid like they weren't even touching themselves.

Bro, you're so right.

Isn't Griffin's dad like, a VP at Sonus somewhere or something?

Well, Regalado's starting libero Griffin Moser is not

typically thought of as the strongest member of their team. Coach Oliver hasn't said why he's out today but his substitute Will Fassen is just incredible. This might be a closer matchup than we thought.

Who let that faggot onto the court?

But Rudy, you wanna look out for Czwartek's serve receive, or what you'd call their defense in other sports.

Griffin's a nepo baby but not with Sonus. His dad is one of Regalado's co-owners.

COVIS made people forget they're supposed to feel ashamed of being desperate and lonely.

One of them's anatomical, the other's social!

Since Six has been starting this tournament, they've never looked more cohesive.

Wait, are you talking about Six and Green's sex tape? Do you have gossip?

Did you see Six's cum face?

The level of nonverbal communication and trust is astounding.

This is why the government started the pandemic.

We're also awaiting more information on a bit of a crisis Six and Green have been tackling this morning. They are looking a little tense but even veterans get some game day nerves.

So I was wondering what the first sport ball was and did some research.

What? You're just making stuff up.

The question is, are they going to choose the smartest play to go up against Regalado?

Once people are forced to acknowledge their death drive, we'll all kill each other so they can say they had nothing to do with it.

And all the scholarship is so wrong.

But that video did not lie. Green's girl pussy is so pretty.

Plus, we're excited to watch this rematch between Six and Green. In case you missed it, here's what happened at last year's tournament.

I, for one, think that clip was just chosen for shock value.

Sport balls are just a conduit for men to experience tenderness.

Why have we been here an hour and the game hasn't even started yet?

No shit, dude. Honestly, bro, intimacy's predictable rules are kind of appealing.

The pre-game is the foreplay of sports!

Enough of that, Rudy, here's Bill Adler with the opening serve.

Did you hear Six cum though?

Mine!

Like, no deep feelings, just squeezing your homie's delicate waist every thirty seconds.

I can't believe we can just watch them having sex. Like forever.

Like it doesn't surprise me that Six bottoms but it would shock me if she doesn't also top.

Short little bursts of performative vulnerability and then disappear before it gets real.

That's why you have to keep your pelvic floor strong!

Where was Six? Did she really let that ball go right between her legs?

Did you see that slomo? Six's shoulders have shoulders.

Maybe she thought it was Green's girl dick coming for her!

And we're back with the third set of the final of the 2021 Sonus Volleyball Tournament.

Mine!

Already? I feel like I don't remember anything from the first two sets!

Rudy Barnes here with one of the all-time greats Tanner Hughes. Czwartek is up 2 sets to none but Regalado's really turned the momentum around. They're up 17–12 but if they don't win, it's over. Auclair with the serve.

And that's an ace!

Oh my god, did you see that serve?

Six looks so nervous.

And it looks like Czwartek's put in a challenge, their first of this set. They're saying the ball was out-of-bounds.

Did you see Charlie just now? Like he's looking for absolution in Luca's crack.

The way Green has kept it together today is so inspiring. Maybe resiliency is real!

Six looks nervous again.

What? His hands barely brushed the waistband.

They could've easily taken the match and now, they've let Regalado gain some momentum.

Well, she's still playing well. But yeah, Czwartek has lost their touch this set.

We definitely paid enough money for it, they better give us five sets.

Mine!

Yeah if Charlie can't grab a cheek between rallies, he won't last.

And it's in! Czwartek loses one of their two reviews.

What if this is it? What if after today they're over it and decide to retire?

Fuck you, ref! That was out!

Sonus pulled out all the stops for this tournament except for the actual tech.

The computer doesn't lie!

Auclair back up to serve. Oh and a float. That's unexpected.

See that graphic they're playing of the ball and its shadow? There's no way its actual imprint on the court was that big and that round of a circle.

What if this is the game that finally forces Six and Green to break up?

Emir's thrown off but it's a pretty slow float, so they have time to get it up.

Like the ball came in at an angle, which means the ball created an oval-shaped impression.

Wait, are Emir's pronouns he/they?

What are you laughing at?

They would never let some game break them up. They've been through so much already, they love each other.

They said 'get it up.'

And Alan puts it down!

Meaning the video review system is fake?

How do I become the person who follows Six around wiping her sweat off the ground?

Alan, the rookie of the team, up for what could be the biggest serve of his career. Czwartek is running out of room. If they don't want to take this to another set, they can't let Regalado side this out.

It's not fake, it's just not real.

If she snapped at me and pointed at the floor, I'd be on my knees so fast.

And he serves it to Green!

Mine!

And she does not give the best pass to Will, who gets the ball in transition but STUFFED! By Six! In her tenth block of the match, the most of any player.

I still think Regalado can come back. So many finals have been won by a three-set turnaround.

Six playing so well today has to be salt in the wound for Green.

Babe!

Green should retire and let her salary go to someone who can actually still play.

Well, they are dating, Rudy, but they're professionals. She's probably disappointed she fumbled that first pass.

Well, she needs to stop showboating and keep her eye on the goddamn ball!

Babe!

But is she mad that it was Six who blocked Ken's attack in particular? Probably not.

Looks like she's blocking just fine to me!

Alan back to serve. And it's back to Green. Much better pass this time!

Exactly. Wanna know how much they make?

BABE! I'm BORED! This is SO PREDICTABLE!

And this time Ken gets it past Six but Emir gets under it. And it's Six again! Off the block!

Sports popularity is driven as much by personality as athletic talent and Six and Green have been building an audience for over a decade.

Even if you have a team to root for, fans of the sport both want this match to go to five sets. But it's clear Czwartek does not.

Oh my god, did you see that?

Her fame may have made the video spread faster, but it also gave her a team of lawyers and publicists or whatever to deal with this crisis. It's not like she's—AHH! Alan just got his first ace!

Look, look they're playing it again!

And they may never admit it, but every one of those boys owes Six and Green their salaries being as high as they are.

Is that Six caressing Alan's wrist AND neck? I want affection like that!

If anything, when you take into account how much NCAL profited from them in college, and how Six and Green made pro volleyball so popular in the States, they're probably still getting underpaid.

Alan, if you fuck this up for Six, we'll know you like to choke.

C'mon, now you're exaggerating. You're saying those two

players are single-handedly responsible? There have to be other stars, other factors, right?

Maybe Six wants to try topping, I mean look at that dainty face of his!

Well, there's Thom and Eric. But two years in a row, their team is shut out of the final again. And would anyone care about them playing in Japan without Six and Green bringing intrigue to volleyball?

Here's Alan, hoping to keep the rhythm after a 4-point run, the longest they've had this set.

Uh, if you're a bottom like Six? If you're a lesbian, like Six? If you're trying to date fellow adults, like Six?

People talk about them as trans icons because that's unique or whatever, but they wouldn't have gotten this far if they weren't also the best in the world at their sport.

But is it worth it though? Green's looked miserable this whole game.

And Regalado keeps it in play.

Wow, just an amazing dig by Six diving out of nowhere.

Regalado is really trying to stop Czwartek's sudden momentum but a bit of a miscue there between Green and Ricky Gomez, so free ball Czwartek.

Top-bottom oppression is hitters getting paid more than liberos.

And Dan dumps it down! We haven't seen him do that yet but especially in a long rally, what a perfect time to catch your opponent off guard.

C'mon, Green, pull it together!

Incredible. Czwartek have brought it back within a point!

You know, Tanner, over the course of this tournament, you've really helped me see the beauty of the dump.

Green's not really having a good day, is she?

Wow, Rudy, you do pay attention! It's become such a trend this week that the opposite teams have sometimes anticipated the surprise dump when the setter telegraphs it. But what a smart disguise from Dan.

Would you if you were her?

We have to talk about Six's incredible dig that kicked this rally into high gear. You know, middle blockers spend most of their time up in the air. Digging is not their main job.

She deserves sweetness too.

But when you can channel that power into a precise dive like that, even the best liberos in the world have got to be impressed.

Do you mean Six or Green?

She's getting it! What, do you think they're not including her?

See how Six's body is actually angled opposite from the ball's trajectory?

Both!

But she's so quick on her feet and gets her torso to change direction so fast!

This is what happens when Asian American masculinity keeps getting threatened by the liberal agenda.

We call those fast-twitch muscles. She only needs two big steps to catapult herself and reach the ball.

Sir, I'm sure getting bullied out of team sports hurt you but it wasn't because you're Asian or bad at sports.

No, this is what happens when trans girls can't take the hormones they want or get the surgeries they want because they'd lose their job.

Rudy, I can't tell you the amount of precise coordination to get under that ball and get it back into play. It's beyond impressive.

GO ALAN!

No, this is what happens when Asians started caring more about healing their bullying trauma than bullying the man.

I love how Tanner's so unashamed of being hot for Six's body.

WHOOSH!

This is a sports event, not a strip club, keep it in your pants!

Alan back up to serve. Can he keep up his streak?

UHHHH! UH UH UH UH OHHH OHHH!

Don't people like spectating sports because it's kind of erotic?

And into the net! Coach Pete has to be happy with that run, though. He'll take one service error after 5 points.

Seriously, there's no pro league that would let them play unless their bodies are exactly as they are.

Damn it! Regalado, I had you down for this. Man up!

C'MON, GREEN!

Well, if they were white, it'd be easier to convince the league to change the rules, right?

Don't worry, there's still time.

Thanks for defining racism, I really needed that!

Yes, Green, whip that ponytail! Fuck, she's so hot.

C'mon, Six! I love you so much!

And Green serves that way long. Not even close, just way too much height on that serve.

Oh shit, Six is serving next?

God, what a day for Asian-on-Asian girl-on-girl t4t crime.

Do you see that smolder? She's so got this.

Team sports are always erotic. You can't put in that effort without telling on yourself.

Kinda weird how all these white people are salivating over these Asian women fighting.

And Six lines up. She can do a float or a heavy hit and usually disguises what she's planning pretty well.

Not as weird as seeing Asians being hot and sporty. I thought I was blazing that trail alone!

So if sports are erotic, are athletes also sex workers?

And a floater AND AN ACE! With her second ace of the set and fifth of the match, she has tied up the game. She is serving so well today!

Should I wear my compression sleeves the way Six does?

Did you see that tape? I thought I was straight before I watched that.

Also, they're not actually fighting. They're just a bunch of pussies flapping their wrists at each other.

So people are just not wearing masks and that announcement was just hygiene pomp fake hype BS?

Whatever! You wish you could taste their pussies. God, Green is so lucky.

You realize that it's not just an aesthetic but customized to Six's body and her injuries, right?

How did you think it was going to be enforced?

Are Alan and Six nuzzling their little nosies? Green is so over.

Yeah, so? It's not that deep.

Let's watch it again. This overhead camera angle really shows what an unpredictable trajectory this type of serve can give the ball.

Six is aiming for that seam right between Green and Luca but manages to catch Regalado off guard.

And Czwartek loves it, Coach Pete with the fist bump.

You have to admit it's kinda genius how they orchestrated a trans homosexual star-crossed lover matchup.

Six back to serve. Now that's a deep breath.

They were never gonna let the league catch them actually arguing?

But it's not, not that deep, you know?

Is Six glaring at . . . Green?

And another floater, a different arc right to the same seam but this time Luca steps into it.

Did you see how they cut that shot! They definitely want it to look like Six and Green are fighting.

You can't help but feel Green and Six have been concocting this elaborate psychosexual drama just for us.

That's caught by Igor, and FROM THE PIPE! And he shoves it down! That's Igor's fourth kill of the set!

Here comes the BOOM!

WOOOOOOO!

I thought I was excited to see them play, but just watching them glare at each other in between sets has me sweating.

So does that make influencers sex workers too?

I feel like Six and Green set back feminism, like, thirty, maybe thirty-five years, at least.

I can't wait for them to make eyes at the bar later.

What a play from Czwartek's Igor. You know when you set up your own setter, your setter's not going to ignore that and we love a good attack from the pipe.

You mean people's reactions to Six and Green set back feminism and anti-racism like, twenty years.

When Green puts her hands on her knees like that, does she know we can see her?

Well, if you think about it, athletes and influencers are selling their bodies and their faces to make money.

And look at Six, faking out Charlie and Luca so that Igor has a pretty clear shot. You know, middle blockers aren't typically the big point getters in a match. But it's such a demanding position.

Did you notice how the commentators aren't really giving Green much play?

They have to go after every single hit like they mean it. But as we just saw Six do brilliantly, a lot of the time, they're faking out the other team's blockers.

Well, Green's not playing well?

No, all workers are selling their bodies, but not all workers are selling the erotic potential of their bodies.

Has Green lost weight?

Six up for her third serve. Normally as you go, you're gonna get more and more aggressive because you can take a bit of a risk.

You're not gonna get a sports drink sponsorship if you don't look good while sweating.

No, I think, she's just that thin.

And a whopper of a serve! One hundred and twenty-six kilometers an hour! That must've hurt but Will's a pro. And through the block from Ken. But Emir's there.

No, I'm serious, I feel like trans women have worked so hard to be taken seriously as women and then Six and Green showed up.

SMACK!

Well, it's not like they face the same threats as most trans people. Or actual sex workers, for that matter. They aren't even selling little personalized videos.

And there's Alan, again! Down the line!

Why are people so hateful? Isn't being nice easier?

No, they're too famous for GuestStar.

It would also make sense if Green's just depleted. If the tournament weren't grueling enough, she's also been doing so much extra media and then that tape dropping this morning.

Would girl internet even exist without Six and Green?

No, being mean is way easier.

You know, he looks so confident today.

It's just all misdirected self-loathing, anyway!

Why are you sobbing?! Nothing's even happened!

Well, Six is too famous for GuestStar.

And Regalado's calling for a review. Let's see what it's for.

If a woman sees a photo of Green promoting a certain lipstick and thinks, If I buy her lipstick, and then maybe that guy will want to put his dick in my mouth, that's kind of—

They're calling for a net touch. I didn't see any movement from the net but we'll see what the computer has to say.

I can't believe these people are just talking about Six and Green like they're some gender specimen. All these perverts just here to jerk off to hot girls and their own arrogant minds.

Green is such a role model for resilience right now. How can she show such courage in the face of such adversity? She's my hero.

Lucy, I love you, but you know you can't say that, right? That's some TERFy transmedicalism bigotry.

So, Tanner, why would a coach call for a review if that obvious sign isn't there?

But they literally pretend to be the opposite sex of what they are so they can have jobs in volleyball. How is that not sex work?

That's sweet but also, Green is just a person like you and me doing her job that she's contractually obligated to do.

Transmedicalism? They're literally just making up words now. Also, we're at a volleyball game, shut up!

So you're sayings Six and Green should just make Lonely-Fans accounts.

Well Rudy, if your player calls for it, they probably saw it.

I love how Six and Green have mass appeal. We need palatable avatars like them for the incremental reforms of the collective mind!

But sometimes you just want to interrupt another team's momentum. If you take them out of play for a minute, you're thinking, hey, maybe they'll come back and overthink a serve.

What? I'm not saying they benefit from male privilege.

But it looks like Green did have a good time using her penis in that tape.

Would you rather have one of Six's stalker fans screaming in your ear?

And look at that, no touch! Regalado is out of video challenges. They're gonna have to hope the calls favor them from here on out.

Better that than those freaks trying to intellectualize a volleyball game!

When the documentary of them finding out about the tape this morning drops, we'll know this was so real.

UHHHH! UH UH UH UH OHHH OHHH!

No, it should be a psychothriller. The opening shot is zoomed into one of their calves, their head out of focus but you can see blood leaking out.

No, but Lucy, you are implying that if other trans people aren't trans in the way you chose to be trans, then they're less trans than you. Girl, that's messed up!

Do you think Six would be offended if I told her she's hot to me because she plays kinda masc?

An incredible comeback. Czwartek have opened up a two-point lead, they're just four away from winning the tournament!

I don't know, I feel like she's said something about being secure enough in her femininity that she's not afraid to claim her masculinity. But do you think you can actually talk to her?

I can't tell if Green looks pissed or just over it.

Six looks calm now as she sets up this serve.

Lucy, are you crying?

Wait where did she say that?

Green said "We need new trans representation" and then gave us a one-woman performance of Trans Victim, Trans Villain, and Trans Whore all in the same week.

Wow, reading all these perspectives really makes you consider all-sides-ism.

In some interview with a magazine, I can't remember which one.

Our icon has range! The way Green is both ahead of her time and so behind it is actually so poetic.

A clever serve from Six but a skillful pickup by Adler.

And Regalado goes up again and WHAT A BLOCK!

I just can't believe you're attacking me. You don't know what I've been through to get that money. That's not fair!

Can you send it to me?

Reading all of your words saved my life. It forced me to lose my ego and accept everything as it is.

That's my baby! Go get this, Green!

So when are you going to make this grand move?

Alan and Six are just having the best day.

Maybe if I see her after the game? I heard all the athletes are staying at the Double Crest.

That's my friend! That's my friend Six!

Here comes the BOOM BOOM BOOM BOOM!

Lucy, what alternative to boy money do Six and Green have access to?

Stop pretending you're friends with them!

Let it go!

LET'S GO!

And Regalado has called a time out.

Wow, do you see Green's coach? He looks pissed!

I wouldn't mind getting spat on by Green's coach.

C'MON, GUYS! Stay in it. This is your set.

Now if you get that set high every time, you're going to give yourself more room.

Seriously? That old guy?

Don't do too much. Clean ball. Shake your nerves off and be patient.

Let's take another look at that picture-perfect block from Alan and Six, what a duo they've made this tournament.

1-2-3! CZWARTEK, CZWARTEK!

Fast knees. Remember your basics, don't get activated.

What? He's in great shape. And he doesn't look so old.

Watch these zones: they're hitting the ball here and here. Watch for the pipe, okay? Now hustle!

1-2-1-2-3! REGA! REGALADO!

Six, back up to serve.

Find the seam, Six!

What are the girls envious of? Man shoulders and a dick that gets hard?

Becoming a sports fan is like watching caterpillars turn into butterflies. Athletes evolve, teams evolve!

And ANOTHER sizzler from Six!

No, that they've been in the public eye for a decade, they look like that, and we've never heard them even mention dysphoria.

It's not just a ball bouncing back and forth over some net. They're selling us the circle of life!

You tore into that seam so good, baby, oh fuck!

Can you hear the white trans girl meltdown happening behind us?

Mine! MINE!

Isn't that just erasing all the people who get permanently injured and retire or the people who get pushed out? Aren't there politics to who gets to play and who gets hired?

And a bulldozer from Ken right at Six but Kenny with the kick keeps it in play. Free ball for Regalado.

Well, yes, the draft is an extra theatrical, public hiring process, but—

Nope? Wait, you mean that girl who does not look white?

And WHAM! What a—and the head referee called it out. But the line judge called it in and looks like he's nodding in agreement with the head ref.

Is it considerate speculation or just violent projection?

Remember that interview in 2017 where Green said she felt no shame about who she was, that was just society? I think we finally broke her!

Regalado's shaking their hands to signal no touch but they're out of challenges, so that'll be another unforced error for them. Seven minutes ago, this was Regalado's set to lose and they've blown it. Czwartek's one point away from match point.

How did all these teams manage to play that close together for the past two weeks and no one got sick?

Right, but she's suffering from a trans identity crisis made up by white queers.

Six is following her teammate Alan with just an incredible serving run. She wants to bring it home.

And it just skims the top of the net but Will's there, he's just so quick on his feet.

Maybe they got some secret vaccine that the rest of us can't access?

Sports are the ultimate canvas. All action, little dialogue, just project whatever fantasy you want!

And saved by Six!

Wait, let me listen more.

And from the pipe! Six! And WILL SAVES IT AGAIN!

So then why don't people engage in like, actual politics or actual life?

Yeah, you should tell that to Green so maybe she'd shut up!

Get it!

Me!

Spectating is not passive! It's all kids have these days.

And Auclair goes for the tip but Kenny's there for an easy pickup.

So you mean sports are like some VR game where people vicariously live out political fantasies through . . . athletes' bodies?

Can you shut up?

And Alan gets it off the hands but WILL IS THERE! Where did he come from?

And their performances too! If sports weren't political, why would states pour money into this?

Oh, you're right. It's that trans people have existed for millennia, except for the ones before modern hormone therapy.

And another easy save from Czwartek. Regalado's unable to make it land and SIX HAS DONE IT!

LET'S GOOO!

She's taken Czwartek to the first of four match points. Surely, they're going to do it. Even if Regalado sides the next one out, they're not going to go on a run long enough to take this from Czwartek.

Not directly but doesn't Sonus receive subsidies and tax breaks? You bet they do!

Regalado's calling a second time out. This is their last one of the set.

That meltdown is just another wave of Six and Green's woman backlash. Let's discuss: Are they annoying because they behave like white girl influencers?

FREEZE! Everybody clap your hands!

Or do we project white girl logic onto them because white people monopolized what queerness looks like?

Well, you already knew that.

Six's serves, including one ace, have led Czwartek on a 7-nothing scoring run. And believe me, it's nothing on Regalado. Everyone's playing incredibly fast, skilled ball.

Either way, we're in this vicious loop where they can't stop overcompensating for the unimaginative public image they can't escape because of accounts like @transaretrans.

Rudy, I have a feeling this match is going to end in the next couple minutes, but I don't want it to.

Either the liberal brainwashing or the sex tape or this match changed my mind. Six and Green, you're just—

It's been such a long season for her. To see Six's confident leadership despite still being the new girl on her team is just so moving to watch.

Wait, what if one of them wasn't trans and just looked like that?

Here we go. And Six, once again, over the net at unbelievable speed.

Calling gender a spectrum was the worst framework!

And on to Green with a beautiful pass.

How do you think it got leaked?

Six and Green prove that trans pettiness will always outweigh trans solidarity, and if we can't get over ourselves, well, maybe . . .

Wouldn't Sonus have the most to profit from the game airing hours after the sexiest scandal of the entire year?

Oh my god!

Whoa.

Anyway, should we introduce ourselves to Lucy? Hey, hottie! Yes, you! I'm Justine.

FINALLY! Something interesting happened.

OH MY GOD!

Fuck! SIX!

This game has been so boring.

Wait, is she okay?

What just happened?

Oh my goodness! Is she all right?

It looks like . . . It looks like Six tripped on the ball itself landing from that triple block. She's grasping her shin, no, her foot, and looks to be in a lot of pain. A freak accident. But is it a real injury or just shock? We'll have to wait and see.

Oh my god, Six. And Green's already there, right by her side. She really does love her.

I thought it was just the boys that faked meltdowns to buy a time-out.

You really can't be shocked it was Green who leaked it.

I can't tell if that's her knee or her ankle.

Let's see if we can get it in slo-mo.

Six just keeps shaking her head.

How many times do you think Six rehearsed fake breaking her ankle? This is peak entertainment.

And if you are, it's because you haven't realized Six is getting fucked by woman who had the gall to try to secure her future during a global collapse.

Just when you thought Six was having a good day.

And she's already being examined by medical staff. It looks like they're evaluating her ankle mobility. Oh dear.

That woman gets PAID to give Six a foot massage? Life isn't fair.

Now that's the richness of trans feminism.

At what point did you think Six was having a good day?

I wish they could give her some privacy.

Alan is having a meltdown.

Then why don't you stop looking?

So selfish, making this about him.

I can't, it's happening right in front of us!

Green seems pretty okay with it.

You didn't watch the tape, did you?

Do you think Green's even paying attention to Alan right now?

Go, Green! C'mon, Regalado!

Of course not!

Then why is this different?

Wait, is she crying?

Wait, what just happened?

Oh my god!

It looks like they're getting her to stand.

YOU CAN DO IT, SIX! Just one more point!

Wow, and we didn't even say that that point went to Regalado.

She's got one arm around Green, and the other around her teammate Alan. In this moment, Green is no longer an opponent, just her girlfriend.

Is she going to put weight on it?

Noooo, SIX!

She's being guided to the sideline hopping on one foot.

Boooo!

Just devastating. Even though Czwartek's only one point away, I know Six wanted to be on the court with her teammates for the win. She has her hands in her face, a towel around her neck, and now an ice pack on her left ankle.

I hope it's just a sprain!

Let's look at the replay: Green sets the ball to Luca who's up against a triple block from Czwartek. He just slips the ball between the players and the net and it lands just next to Six's feet. When the block comes down, Dan jostles into her so she slips on the ball and rolls it.

It's probably just a sprain or a twist. If it were anything else, don't you think she'd be on her way to the hospital right now?

And it'll be Sam Friedan subbing in for Six. He's been

out all tournament for an injury but it looks like Coach Pete thinks he can at least handle a couple rallies. He looks a little tentative.

I wouldn't put it past Sonus to require her to be on the court for the duration of the game, you know, just so she's visible.

So there's nothing Six could've done to prevent this?

Do you think Green set up the play for this to happen?

Bruh, have you seen Six's cross-training routine? We know her ankles are sturdy. Sometimes these things just happen. You trip the wrong way or step weird.

You mean you think she wanted to injure her partner? What the hell is wrong with you?

And it'll be Luca Bianchi to serve. He's gotta send something strong so his team can score this point to keep Regalado in the game.

I mean like, maybe Green wanted—

If anything, I'll bet Six's strength prevented this from being worse.

EVERBODY, CLAP YOUR HANDS!

Did she perform for the public or did the public perform her for itself?

The referees seem to be conferring about something. There hasn't been a review but they're delaying the serve.

—are you serious? Is there a reason you think she could be that conniving?

Now, what's happened to Six is obviously terrible and even if you're on team Regalado, you gotta feel bad that this happened to her.

It's the setter's job to set up the attacker and the set Green gave Luca—

One hundred percent, Rudy.

Like you can't just plan these things. That was an accident!

Well, they're playing each other, they've been scoring against each other all season.

But at the same time, is part of them wondering whether this has knocked Czwartek off its game enough to where they can actually swing it back?

You ever think about how when men have sex, their buddies ask them if they scored?

Six looks on in tears as the referees give Luca the go-ahead. Green is really going to have to focus if she wants to get this back.

Nobody uses that euphemism anymore.

Still. Ball sports are all about conquest and demarcating territory.

Well, you know, even at this stage of a match, you're not supposed to give up.

Babe, let's go! I want to beat the rush!

Even if you think you'll lose, you'll still try and close the gap as much as you can, even if just to soften the blow. But now, can Regalado get their hopes up?

God, Sonus must be thrilled. Can you imagine how this looks on TV right now?

Look at that playback of Six falling on the big screen! She looks like she did on that tape when Green made her cum!

This is stressing me out.

Oh my god, is your phone background seriously a screenshot of their sex tape? That's so sick!

If your opponent's weaker, your innate competitive drive has to see it as an opportunity.

Can you send it to me?

###

In Yemma's telling, Six and Green's careers had been marked by three pivotal memes: the first (Green's sweet bubbly cheeks) drew attention to their trailblazing arcs in collegiate sport; the third (Six and Green kissing through the net a year ago) elicited a fresh wave of horny hope for romance in the early pandemic.

The second meme bridged their collegiate volleyball fame to a broader internet celebrity only possible in the mid-2010s. Six and Green called it the foot-flop meme. In Green's second season with Regalado, a slo-mo replay showed her body hurtling into the air for a rare spike. Setters didn't usually spike and shouldn't try to sneak one in too often or otherwise the play became predictable, like the dump was during the 2021 Sonus Tournament. But four years ago, Regalado was up two sets to none. Green didn't need to make the move. But as she jumped up to back set a particularly high ball, she saw how the opposite team was just waiting, their arms slack and their feet firmly on the ground. During the replay, Tanner exclaimed, And out of nowhere, Green just twists her torso and THWACK! gets an easy kill because her opponent underestimated her. The camera looked up at Green's piked body.

Her feet hung loose and fluttered violently from her slackened ankles as she hit the ball. Like most sports memes, it was an otherwise unremarkable display of standard skills. This was just Green having a little fun at her job.

But of course, one fan, a wholly unremarkable pervert, noted the black sock tugged up Green's shin. He saw Green's ankle flopping in a shoe that dazzled in the flash and found it so erotic. He burned the clip into his retinas and logged onto a little website embedded with a rudimentary video editor. Atop the five-second clip, he overlayed the words *1st Base* in the empty space between Green's open mouth and the ball. When Green's thin wrist and wide hand made contact with the ball, the man overlaid *2nd Base* above the net. Finally, as Green's ankles flopped about, he placed *3rd Base* next to her toes. He logged on to social media and posted his meme with the caption "Just take me to 3rd Base, Daddy @everyourgreen."

As meme connoisseurs had long ago noted, a meme's cleverness had little correlation to its engagement. Rather, factors like the sauciness of the rest of the feed and the general mood of casual browsers dragging at sensitized glass were more significant if harder to measure. Any random person could publicize his average horniness on a public account. But crucially, a person with more followers saw the foot-flop meme, felt his crankiness subside at the unexpected image, and so, decided to refleet it.

From there, more followers breathing the same virtual malaise had a laugh at the embarrassing humor and mixed-metaphorical earnestness. It took off because it was taking off. Average people who knew nothing of volleyball shared it privately, reposted it publicly, and debated what the sexual volleyball bases really were and what made this meme noteworthy. Or not.

In the volleyball world, it was huge. Green Live Grin-laughed it off around other players. She was privately horrified as she saw a new horde of volleyball fans follow her. That quickly shifted to a private thrill as an even larger horde of random strangers followed her and tagged her in their iterations of it. One edited a donut above first base, a plain croissant by her hand, and a basket of mini muffins by Green's feet. The caption read "circles of pastry hell." Green did not think it was very good but laughed because there she was, the majestic overlord of someone's fantasy carb inferno.

In other iterations, people Photoshopped male celebrity faces atop Green's. The online queers cried out about trans erasure and made their own iterations with trans celebrity faces, which did not gain as much traction. Seeing new strange queer people claim her felt flattering and disconcerting. Did they care about volleyball or just that she was a Groundbreaking Trans? Plus Hot.

Now they would become even more famous. Infamy was the most reliable catalyst and the sex tape would spread forever, like a virus that didn't need to mutate to survive. Even if it eventually languished in many a forgotten phone motherboard, all the metaphysical fantasies of Green would persist. Green hadn't always needed an improv coach. But being undeniably over-memeified compared to Six had messed with her.

Nearly a year into their work with Guthrie, she felt like she was finally relearning how to be a person.

Until today. Six, as the tape's surprise bottom, somehow got to be somewhat more of a person and Green felt like a cartoon again. Yemma and Brent had prepared them for their personal brands evolving beyond their control and yet, they hadn't. They couldn't get them out of the post-awards reception either. Phil had really, really wanted them there. Players and staff and sponsors all milled about, strategizing whose autographs they wanted, whose inner diva they wanted to tease with the fantasy of a future transfer or brand deal.

I can't believe today happened, Green said from her highboy. The polyester peach tablecloth was hideous.

Me neither, Six said, hunching on one leg in her sequined mini-dress. She wished she had packed a less gaudy backup outfit.

I'm really proud of you.

Oh. For what?

Green, in a dark emerald palazzo pant and matching oversized blazer, kept her gaze on her partner, thinking of the braced ankle hidden below. You've played so well this tournament. You've been so strong.

Six tried to hear what Green was affirming for her. She said, I'm proud of you too. You've really found a way to cope with everything, not just for yourself but for so many people all over, all while playing our silly sport. You've been tireless, it's—hi!

I just wanted to say, Walt began, her eyes looking just left of Six's face, I'm so sorry about your ankle, that sucks. But you totally deserved MVP. You've been incredible this tournament, and for the sport, Six.

Thanks, Walt. That's really nice of you, but I didn't die. It's just a sprain, I'll be back so soon.

Hi, Walt, Green said. Hey, Alan. Good game today.

Thanks! Alan said as he walked right past Green to grab Six's shoulder. Six, seriously, you're so inspiring. I'm so thankful for you.

Aw, thanks. Six accepted probably Alan's fifth hug of the evening. He'd been almost more emotional about Six's injury than Six was. Before Phil even announced that Six had won MVP and Best Middle Blocker, Six had to tell Alan to relax.

When you fell, Alan continued, I was like, Oh my god, Six saved my first pro season and I couldn't save you. You could've died!

Walt's jaw dropped.

Alan, there wasn't an incel with a gun looking for me, just a stray ball. Six patted Alan on the shoulder in a not *not* maternal way.

Six, don't joke like that. Alan's face was agape. Do you need anything when we get back home? Want me to get your luggage at the airport?

Alan, you sweetheart. Tournaments really were like summer camp. Every day felt like a déjà vu of the day before, the same people gathering with not much new to remark upon. Except Six's naked fornicating body had zipped through every ethernet cable and light-emitting diode across the globe and her ankle had sprained. And still, she had to keep petting Alan on the head.

Green eyed Alan doting on her girlfriend before eyeing Walt looking sheepishly at her. Why was Walt's crush less fun and more awkward than Alan's crush? Another thing Six had that Green didn't. Had either of them seen the sex tape?

Ladies! What a fucking day you two have had!

Oomph! Six grunted.

It was Henry, picking up Six from behind and squeezing her to his chest, and Curtis, who gave a less infantilizing hug to Green. Walt took another step away from the circle.

Really, Curtis elaborated. From you both winning awards and Six winning two, to that sex tape to another dramatic conclusion to a tournament final and this horrid injury. What can't a girl do?

That would make a great vlog cold open, Six said.

Henry put her down gingerly. He should've known better than to underestimate them. From college to Aracaju, he'd always been above average but had never been given the acclaim of more boisterous outside hitters who made themselves stars.

Mind if I get quote from you, actually? Curtis said.

Henry was sad Six was injured, obviously, but disappointed that Six and Green were displaying a resiliency any trauma therapist would drool to make a case study out of.

Six beamed as she regrasped the table beneath that flame-retardant slick. Of course. Do you want me to talk about fornication or ankle instability? She turned to see Green crying silently.

I'm so exhausted, Green moaned, as if just realizing it.

Six tried to hop around the table to hold her but only made

it two scoots before tripping on Alan's feet. Crutches were so impractical for a cocktail party.

Here, let me. Alan swooped in. He put his arm behind Six's back and gently guided her close to Green, who was leaning her head on Curtis's shoulder. Henry patted Green's shoulder and tried to revel in his minor victory. He was an outside, the most versatile player. He'd keep making plays behind the scenes. No celebrity lived long these days.

Walt stepped forward, his mouth quivering with emotion. Or speech?

What was with everyone? Six wondered. And then, What if Walt leaked it? Was that why he'd been so awkward?

I'm sorry, Green dribbled. It's just, when we went to sleep last night, she gestured to Six, we knew today was going to be a big day but it wasn't supposed to be this big.

I'll catch y'all later, Walt said, and speed-walked out of the banquet hall.

I know, Henry said gravely. Especially after the murders a couple weeks ago. Asian trans girls have been so violated.

A day ago, Six and Green were depleted from what it had taken them to reach the final, but still functional. Tonight, they had nothing left. The tournament had ended. They hadn't done their usual post-game media or fan meet-and-greets. But they would hold a press conference the next day to assert their narrative.

As for this smaller, contained circuit of their colleagues, when else but now would they get to show their togetherness? Everyone who had seen their pussies or heard about their pussies needed to congratulate Six and Green so they could remember they'd been there when the superstar sluts were still stunned. At least Yemma and Brent had made sure Phil announced that Six and Green would not be taking selfie requests. Tonight's photos would be pivotal to narrating this scandal. Selfies told the world they were accessible. If Six and Green would be the first search result for *volleyball* for the foreseeable future, their official photos would show them to be glamorous and untouchable.

###

An hour later, they lay on Six's hotel bed in sweats and in silence. Green's eyes were closed. She was as tired as she could be without being sleepy. Just next to her, Six was curled over her own body, eyes fully open.

Yemma and Brent had encouraged Green and Six to let them take care of the fallout. But then Green had seen what they were saying. And now, she could finally ask the question that had poked at her all afternoon: Can you believe people think I released it?

What? Beanie. Are you serious? Six reached for her phone but then caught herself. What? Why! But you didn't! Of course you didn't!

Of course not, Green said calmly. Six's indignation on her behalf was so affirming.

So why? Six sat up, her face stunned.

Because, Green said, still lying down, Apparently I'm secretly an ambitious domme top girlboss who's been trying to co-opt last week's murders of Suzy Akhter, Clarisse Valdez, and Bea Tran into my own influencer empire.

Green! How can people say that? Six's surprise felt less sincere now.

I can't believe people can see my little cunt. Whenever they want.

Oh, Green, I know.

My dysphoria's been less distracting over the last year, with you, and now, hearing everyone talk about my shoulders and my nipples has brought it all back.

Green, I—

And that people are going to use my pussy and how we use our bodies together as proof that I'm fake. Green began crying again.

I know, baby, the transmisogyny is so deep.

So you haven't seen? Green said.

No, Six said, lying back down. You know I haven't. Especially today of all days, why would I?

This whole tournament has been so exhausting. I thought I was underperforming all week, but today? Six. I played so bad. She cried harder.

As Green's tears continued to blot the hotel sheets, Six pulled Green's slackened body to her and pressed her to her chest. Are people saying anything about me?

Not really. Hardly anyone's accusing you of doing it. Green sniffled. They're just shocked you're bottom or whatever. Or shocked that other people are shocked. A lot of people feel bad for you, like they're embarrassed for you.

Ah, another version of transmisogyny.

Six scooted back, forgetting her bad foot as Green slid across it. Ow, fuck!

Green stayed snuggled between Six's arms, not responding to Six's comment or her cry of pain. Her mind rewound the scroll of her screen and heard catty voices reading all the worst comments aloud.

Six let her ankle's throb subside in silence. She wondered if Green had heard her and if she had, whether she had registered what Six had said, and if she had, whether she had anything to say, any support to offer. Green may have appeared to be topping Six in that one video, but when was Six not the big spoon?

Do you think my reputation is ruined? Green asked. While she'd gained 100k new followers, she'd also lost 30k old ones. She didn't have access to Six's analytics but knew that her net gain was 120k followers. Now that the world knew that Six had that in her, even more people were enraptured. By her. And Six truly couldn't be bothered.

What do you mean? Six responded, her annoyance still in stealth mode. Last night wasn't the night to get into it, and tonight would be even worse. They should just sleep, have a fuller debrief when they weren't both deep-fried and burnt. But Green still had more to share.

Like, if everyone thinks I leaked the video and that I'll do anything to get ahead and that I'm a slut and that I'm a conniving bitch who injured you on purpose like that gymnast did in—

Wait, what?

—is my credibility shot? Green nuzzled her head into Six's neck, her hair tickling Six's nose, which twitched in response.

Green, what are you talking about? Who's saying that?

You know. People.

Six shook her head and closed her eyes. Maybe she would have to acknowledge that the voices online were real after all.

So, do you think I'm ruined?

Maybe Six was babying her, but Green was being childish. Green, darling, we're famous. Six kept her voice even as her exasperation began to spill out. Someone somewhere is always going to think we're being fake. That's before the transmisogyny. And the racism! We all know you didn't injure me. Sonus loves you, Regalado loves you, any real sports fan is so proud of you for playing on today and—

Yeah, but you won MVP, Green mumbled.

Six gently slid Green's body off hers so she could feel her throat get hot from her words alone. She could no longer wait another day. Green. Are you serious? What's the matter with you?

As Green felt the staticky comforter against her back, she realized she'd said too much. I—I'm sorry. I didn't mean it. She had never seen such disgust on her girlfriend's face before.

Yeah, Six said. I actually think you did. Which is fine. But can you own up to it so we can talk about it?

I, I'm just, I'm just hurt, I'm scared. I won one trophy but you won three.

Green, what's this about? Are you jealous of me?

No, I . . .

Six could've raised an eyebrow but she did not move her face.

What's gonna happen to us? Our careers! You're injured, we're getting—

Oh, so you remembered. Six rolled her eyes, as if waiting till now to express her vexation played no part in Green getting so ridiculous.

What's that supposed to mean? Green scooted up on her elbows.

Green, you're great at gassing me up when good things happen. But sometimes I feel like you don't listen to me or don't know how to acknowledge when I'm hurting too.

What? Where is this coming from? Green's face looked genuinely shocked. Six had been so supportive all tournament. Like when?

Green's curiosity felt like an opening but it also made Six suspicious, which she didn't like for herself or for Green. She didn't want to be another troll who thought her girlfriend's every move was postured. But sometimes trust was sustained through action instead of feeling. This was her Green. She had to keep going.

Just now.

Huh?

Just now, you accidentally slid on my foot and I cried out and you didn't say anything. And when I said people's comments about me in the video are transmisogynistic too, you didn't acknowledge it. It's like you're so caught up in yourself, you're not even listening. Are you actually worried about us or just yourself?

Green couldn't remember the last time she'd heard such passion from Six that wasn't a proclamation of affection for her. Why had she chosen this moment to reveal that she'd been this upset? How had she not noticed that her girlfriend was this upset?

I'm sorry. I'm so tired, I didn't even register what you'd said.

I'm tired too! I'm sad and embarrassed and pissed! And I also got injured today. But I'm trying to pay attention to you.

I'm sorry. Green reached over and rubbed Six's knee. But you're making this sound like this is a pattern.

But Green, it is! Six didn't brush Green's hand away but she didn't reciprocate the gesture either. She went on, Remember when I was sick and you were more concerned about our live show? When I brought it up, you were more worried about disrupting the score—

But you said—

Let me finish! Six cut back in.

Okay! Green withdrew her hand and leaned into the headboard.

That night didn't have to be a huge deal. But then, we flew here for the tournament. Six looked in Green's eyes, hoping to see some sort of recognition. She willed herself to stay calm. I was talking about feeling anxious and spirally about playing our sport during a pandemic. And you couldn't just hear me out!

Okay, but Six, we were about to take off! Also, you were accosted by one of your millions of fans!

But you didn't have to be so dismissive. When we got here and the murders happened, I made space for you. I listened. Six waved her arms frantically. And you didn't acknowledge that I had wanted to talk about it too! You didn't connect the dots! And the first day of the tournament. I woke up with that awful headache and you haven't asked me once if it's come back.

I just figured. Well, that you're like . . . Green shrugged, the gesture both sheepish and dismissive.

That I'm like what? Six asked, her face triumphant.

You're so strong and so easygoing. Like if you were actually sick or really stressed, I thought I'd know.

So even to you, I seem tougher. More butch. More masc.

That's not what I said.

And even if you didn't mean it, did you realize you just implied it? Six asked coolly.

Rather than making Green feel guilty, Six's even, knowing tone made Green feel more defensive.

No, honestly, I'm sorry if you felt like—I mean I thought we said that dynamic was reductive.

Six pretended she didn't hear that non-attempt at an apology. Doesn't mean it's not happening between us.

True, Green said, but then pressed on, But you are tougher. Is it my fault for believing it's just easier for you to be so strong? You show me all the time how unphased you are.

But we've just been talking about moments where I was telling you I was very phased. Six threw up her arms. And you're my girlfriend. You're my partner. Just because I can be a rock doesn't mean you should assume I'm just a rock.

You're right, I shouldn't. Green said. I'm sorry. But why did you bottle so much up before talking to me about this? Why didn't you connect the dots if you saw them so plainly?

Green, it feels like it's always me connecting the dots. It's always me doing the work of tending to not just you, but our relationship. But I feel like everything we've said about the video has been about how hurt and humiliated you are. I'm hurt and humiliated too! And it feels worse that you can't even think to consider my feelings.

Whether in response to Six's words or her voice breaking, Green's face sank, her chest deflated. Even more than the tape or the trophies, it was this moment when she felt like she could actually lose everything. Her girlfriend. Her career. She had to fix this. Solemnly, she said, That makes sense. I really didn't mean to put you in that dynamic. Because you do, do so much for us. Six, I'm so sorry. For not caring for you the way you always consider me. I'll look out for you more closely.

Finally. An unqualified apology. The plainness of her expression moved Six. She loved Green after all. A quiet voice in Six's heart still wondered how much of Green's regret was genuine and how much was derived from Guthrie's coaching. Six had wanted to integrate their real life into the show but now the specter of the show was creeping into their relationship. This really was too meta and Six was not equipped to guide them through the tangle.

Can I ask something? Green said.

Oh no. She was asking for permission now.

Sure.

Can you tell me what you need, when you need it? I can connect some dots but I'm not a mind-reader. If I'm being a self-obsessed diva, can you just interrupt me? She squeezed Six's fingers between one hand and caressed her scalp with the other. Little lady. Do you want to share more about how you're feeling?

Yeah, Six said. I'm not upset that it's a video of you fucking me. It's that they can see us so vulnerable. Anybody with an internet connection gets to label our intimacy like they know us. And because everyone expects me to lose it, I have to play along with their cis-normie sexual taxonomy. I feel like people take it for granted that I'm more expressive, but really, I've just felt so alone today.

Baby, I know, Green said. Especially when we're far apart, I only get limited information about how you're doing. I'm sorry for not being more attentive. She paused. But it's not on me to vocalize your feelings or to know when you don't mean what you say in front of other people.

But isn't it a little bit?

Green exhaled. They were circling, like a never-ending rally.

Six pouted. She knew that arguments weren't meant to be won, and yet she kept pushing. It'd be easier if you spent less time distracted by your phone, she said. I feel like even when I see you, you're more concerned with them than with me.

Green blinked. Six knew with certainty that Guthrie had perfected this gesture with her.

You mean I should spend less time doing our other job?

But she couldn't fault Green for it either. Maybe she had to let Green's self-expression evolve. Guthrie always said you could imbue anything with sincere intention.

Green, our main job already takes care of us.

So less time uplifting our communities? And just enjoy our money and volleybro company?

You know I so admire you for all the extra energy you're able to give. But at a certain point . . . Six exhaled. She was so delirious. How much of a difference can you really make?

Green made her face righteous. She knew Six must've felt this way given her complete indifference to her follower count. But she'd never heard her say it aloud. Six, she said. People are dying and losing access to resources every day. We have a social responsibility to use our platforms to sway public opinion and build resistance.

Six made sure her whine was cute and funny and, also, serious. But we can't help the revolution if we're burnt out. We have to take care of each other. When we're together, is it too much for you to just be with me? I know I'm being needy. But I've missed you.

Clobbered as she was, Six could still deliver a nuanced, argument-ending statement. She noticed Green let the air calm before responding, something she hadn't always done. Athletes knew better than anyone how to hone a skill.

Green sighed. I love you. I've just been craving connection with our people since the murders. It's hard to balance with travel and our silly SpaceTimes. But we can shift things. You make space for me because I take up space and time. Help me make some for you.

Ugh, we sound like a goofy ad for SpaceTime. Six covered her eyes with the edge of her delicate forefinger. We should ask Brent and Yemma to see about a sponsorship or something.

Ha, right. Or for WellSpace. Green grimaced.

Their discussion had escalated and deescalated so quickly. Recentering Team Six and Green couldn't really be this easy, could it? Maybe Six had been overthinking. Maybe Green would be more aware. Maybe their foundation was strong enough to just take these notes aboard and move on. They'd received daily feedback from coaches for close to two decades. Maybe a career in sports had paid its dividends in life lessons too. Maybe years from now, they'd look back at this awful day as a brutal test that ultimately brought them closer together.

Green said, I'm just scared. What happened to you today is one of my biggest nightmares. I know we're making good money now, but what if your injury had been worse? What happens when we retire? What can I realistically do after this? Like it's so gross, but as we're getting our brand out there in light of everything, I can't help but think about how this could help us plan for our future.

The future is scary, Six said. Glad I got to live out your worst fantasy for you.

Six! Stop it. Green swatted at Six's arms before resting a hand on her bare leg.

No, thank you. For all the moves you make for us. She paused. But now, whatever we do from here, no one's going to talk about us without that asterisk of our little tape. I was reading Tricia's article and she said something about how, like, careful we are with our bodies and our platforms. That sounds foreboding now, doesn't it?

They'd been awake for fifteen hours already and were both

just about out of thoughts. Green tapped her fingers on the back of Six's neck and Six let Green's touch soothe her spine.

But then Green remembered what Tricia wrote too. Honestly, the *Pacific* profile already feels so outdated. How could we have said any of that and meant it? Having to play after this morning already cut something off in me but thinking about that article makes me feel even more embarrassed. I don't know what I'm supposed to think of myself. Why be trans at all if being trans is like this?

Six's thoughts hadn't yet veered in this direction.

Could we possibly be anything else but trans? Six said. The emotion in her voice made her insipid question so affecting, Green's eyes teared up again. A beautiful enough girl could dissolve existential despair.

Six pressed her body against Green and kissed her. The warmth of her neck brought more tears to her eyes. Green felt the wet on her cheeks and turned around. Her lips tingled as she kissed back. Six leaned her head against Green. Six wanted to keep lightening the mood: Can you imagine what they'd say if we of all people detransitioned?

A flurry of comments and sound bites assembled in Green's mind.

Two boys decide that they are, indeed, really, in fact, just boys! Luckily they won't need breast reduction surgery, Six said with pompous bravado. Coming up at 8:00, should all trans people just be sent to the asylum?

Green laughed and tried to play along. You promised me! You lied! It was all a publicity stunt, she said, her voice unable to fully commit as tears continued to fall. So. You've made quite an impression on Alan's pro development.

Six grinned sheepishly. He's the sweetest. We just get each other on the court, you know? Like the Six-th sense is really strong there. And yes, I think the poor thing probably has some confused crush on me.

Probably? That little puppy will follow us home if you don't stop him.

Greenie, baby! Is this you, jealous?

Should I be? She leaned over and gave Six another kiss. Also, this is another semi-straight bro thing I don't get. How do you use your body to communicate like a bro while being the only woman on the team? Without being threatening?

Like I'm not gonna beat them up? Six winked.

Like you're not gonna all of a sudden come on to them. Their worst nightmare!

Well, maybe not Alan's. Six smirked again.

Sixy! Green slapped Six's chest playfully and rested her hand above her heart.

Did you miss just cradling my titty like this?

Yes. Green smiled, I did.

Six reached her arm and found the bottom ridge of Green's ribcage and squeezed, like she knew she liked.

Babe, I think the problem is that you really are more woman than me. That's not a self-loathing thing to say, is it?

Six! Green said, now with mock-outrage face. Sometimes irony said what earnestness couldn't.

But like, why do people get so worked up about how woman-y woman we are?

Because we make more money than most of them.

Ahh, Six said. So they have to lay us bare and naked in front of the entire public internet.

Exactly! To put us in our place!

Now that they were talking about it, they'd have to keep talking about it. Green asked, Do you think we'll ever find out who did this?

I don't know. I don't think so, honestly. Six sighed.

What if it was someone on one of our teams?

What if it was a rival coach just trying to make a point?

What if it was a rando stalker hacker?

What if it was someone who works for Czwartek or Regalado's marketing and knows exactly how much more we make than them? Wait. What if it was Phil?

Phil? Green asked, her face stunned.

For Six, Green's shock was confirmation. Her brain was totally sharp again. Hear me out: Phil's background is in pro-wrestling but somehow he's marketing volleyball? What would you do—reinvent the wheel? No, you do what's always worked. Wrestling's not about the fighting in the ring. You need a controversy so you can make everyone talk about it. What if releasing those videos are part of his hype-building strategy?

Oh my god. That's extra disgusting. You think?

I don't know, Six said. Maybe he hacked the arena Wi-Fi when our phones were syncing with the cloud. Just something about his sympathy for us at the gala felt so fake, like so rehearsed, like he knew something.

I know what you mean! Green patted Six's knee

emphatically. It was like, Is he winking at us? Is it because he's watched the video?

True. Maybe it's just that.

Poor Six and Green. They were so far off.

Also, I wanna sleep, but my foot.

Aw, Sixy, do you need anything? Ice?

No, I'm good. Six beamed. Thanks, sweetie.

Green continued their collective thought, If only we could actually sleep and not feel like we have to make sense of this right away so that we can explain what it means to our public.

Green, babe, don't tell me they want more from us.

Six, I scrolled for like a minute, and even if I hadn't, what do you think?

Yemma and Brent had released their joint statement in the middle of the final so that Six and Green wouldn't be distracted by it. But even when wishing them well, Six's and Green's followers were ravenous for more than polite professionalism. They wanted Six and Green to share their genuine feelings. They wanted theater.

Six wondered how soon she could face her phone again. Now that we've had our own lesbian processing talk, should we try and at least lie down?

I'm already literally there, what are you talking about? Green wanted to delete the part of her brain that also grieved the realization that she'd never catch Six's follower count now. She just was not that girl.

Six rubbed Green's back as she rolled over. I'm gonna cut the lights.

And as Green reached over to set her phone alarm, she saw it. As ever, it was Green, not Six, who saw it first. She did play with him—well, her, and also, played? Six, she said.

What?

Walt is trans!

Wait, what?! Are you serious? Six sat up. Is that still her name?

No! I mean, yes! She said she thought about it but is committed to maintaining continuity in her sense of self with her name as she's—

Is that supposed to be a dig at us?

And she's quitting the league.

What? Did you know?

No! She's never given any hint. She's starting HRT and gonna skip a season before trying to join the women's league.

Wait, for real?

Yes! Green bit her lip. She was hoping Six would say it.

Oh my god! That's . . . incredible! In the dark, Six's voice sounded shocked but genuinely excited.

Green knew Six wouldn't say it. Not Six, the affable angel. Green was the cold shrew who thought things like, But *we're* the trans girls in pro volleyball.

She really never said anything? No hint? She hasn't reached out to you?

No text or anything! I guess he, I mean, she's acted odd all tournament. But I never thought much of it? Oh my god, was that egg girl behavior? Not just socially awkward Asian boy behavior?

Slippery slope, I guess.

Green waited. She really didn't want to say it, not aloud! But it was 2:00 a.m. and her self-restraint was long gone. Now we're actually gonna have to compete with her?

And then she had another important question. Wait, is she growing her hair out?

###

Trans girl Walt watched the trans comments and trans followers flash across her trans-owned portable phone. She gulped and then choked in her trans throat. She'd forgotten to take trans deep breaths.

She hadn't even trans-come out to the Regalado coaching staff yet.

She quickly opened her trans email and pasted part of her trans Instagraph post caption, which she'd spent the past few hours drafting and trans tweaking. She scrolled through and trans typed a quick *sorry for the short notice* and a *thank you so much for everything*. She remembered to copy her agent, whom she also hadn't told, and hit *Send*.

She pulled measured cylinders of air through pursed lips and rolled over and opened the forums and began thinking about making her first post when she saw that someone had already beaten her to it. The subject read: "Walt Park – ANOTHER pro trans girl men's volleyball player."

They were talking about her. She could never post now. If it weren't for Six and Green, these people wouldn't have found out about her so quickly. They were excited she was actually transitioning. Okay, someone corrected, that she had found the courage to both socially and medically transition. It just hit her. What if microdosing toward biological womanhood made her slower? Less aggro when she needed to be an aggro lady on the court? Walt didn't even have a doctor yet.

The forum hoped she'd be able to find her way onto a women's team, though knew she'd have a harder time than Six or Green. Cis boys occasionally liked to condescend to let girls in the boys' club, for show obviously, but cis girls loved to gatekeep the girls' club even more, someone wrote. Walt didn't know anyone who worked for the women's league but she did know a couple of volleygal players. She hadn't told any of them before either. Maybe she'd switch positions. With the shorter net, maybe she could be a hitter or even a middle like Six.

She opened Instagraph again and looked at her post. It was a photo she'd taken minutes ago. She had squeezed herself into the blue velvet dress she'd packed but hadn't been brave enough to actually wear to the closing gala. She put on the makeup she'd hidden in her checked luggage. After congratulating Six and Green, she fled from the gala in frustration. She finally realized she'd always be feeling rejected and dejected if she kept trying to be seen by them like this. No one was going to just look her in the eye and just know. She knew it was hasty but sometimes rash decisions were the only way. Her hand shook so much that it'd taken four tries to get her eyeliner right.

The resulting mirror selfie took only one try. She stood

in three-quarter profile, her left leg long in front of her but bent at the knee. She looked a little square in the torso but her torso was still kind of square. From the pearlescent studs to the plain dress and heeled combat boot, she deployed the unspoken visual codes that she was Trans Woman. And finally, she thought she looked good.

She'd fuss over logistics later. It didn't matter if she succeeded or was pretty or if her skin acquired the trans facelift once she started taking estrogen. She could just get a facelift if she needed. Now she had her own flock of transphobic haters trying to commandeer the narrative of her comment scroll. But to her, it seemed the fans congratulating her blared louder. Now that she'd told everyone she was going to try, she had no choice but to. This post would hold her accountable.

She sank deeper into her bed. She couldn't actually feel a weight lifted, could she? No, she couldn't be that tacky. Still, as she looked down at her naked body, knowing that it was now trans to all people who cared to know, she thought it looked more trans to herself. How lovely a woman she was.

###

It's not just that we're trans women, Six (@sixsosweet, 1.4 million followers) was saying. We're trans women who don't quote-unquote pass. She waved her hand as if swatting away the transphobia. We don't want to pass. We don't need anyone to approve our womanhood.

Girls like us were never meant to belong in a society like this, Green (@everyourgreen, 1.1 million followers) continued, We've been thinking a lot about those tragic murders and the really horrific invasion of privacy we experienced a few weeks ago.

Seated side by side in Green's living room, they looked straight into the camera. The murderer was formally charged but Six and Green weren't expecting justice. They still had no idea who had released the tape.

Six went on, As I've been recovering from this injury, we've been reflecting on why we do what we do. It hasn't been easy. But we're so thankful you're here.

We've been talking about how people want us to feel like less than them because they feel threatened that we're more. We know who we are. Regarding next season, all we have to say for now is we look forward to continue beating people at their own game.

Guthrie had reassured them that this announcement could and maybe should sound as prepared as the statement they'd filmed for Sonus. It could and should repeat some of the already tired talking points they had used with *The Pacific* and countless times over their career. By making the performance reveal itself, they let their audience know that they knew. Everything devolving in the world around them, combined with such a destabilizing end to their season, helped them find a way forward, willfully and deliberately. There was no pure path.

We're so thankful for your energy and support around this announcement. I'm so glad we finally get to share this with you. We're launching 6&G Moves, a new platform in partnership between Green, myself, and Sonus. Six's petite claps were so cute. Her phone displayed a flurry of clap images floating up the screen as they broadcast live to over ninety-six thousand screens worldwide.

Green's eyes lit up and she clapped too. 6&G Moves is a new hub for uplifting trans athletes of all levels. From exclusive workout tips to virtual self-defense classes led by us, we're building a real community for trans athletes, of all ages, races, and abilities, whether for professional, amateur, or recreational sports. 6&G Moves will offer so many ways to train, find friendship, and grow stronger. Together.

Swipe up to download our app, subscribe to our newsletter, donate to support scholarships for trans athletes, or attend one of our upcoming clinics. We'll also be launching a 6&G Moves podcast, where we'll discuss the past, present, and future of gender and sports. Our first episode drops next week with special guest Walt Park! Six said, pointing to the bottom of the frame.

Green could picture all the people voting for them with their dollars. At 6&G, we believe that if the last year and a half has taught us anything, it's that finding ways to think expansively about moving in our bodies, to actively create the transformation we're always craving for ourselves, is so fundamentally crucial to not just living safely, but to living a vibrant life.

We love you all so much and are so thankful you've decided to follow along on our journey.

We'll both be taking a break from posting regularly on social media,

But you can look forward to exclusive content coming soon on 6&G Moves,

The strongest movement begins from the center.

Good morningnight!

Good nightmorning!

For a second longer, before the episode shut off and their screens went blank, thousands of viewers felt it. The conviction radiating from Six and Green's faces and refracting onto their retinas was theirs too. Now that was female empowerment.

###

Assists

Near my last deadline, I watched volleyball on TV and was moved to tears. It was more slow trickle than full sob, and I was definitely wiped. But I still found the sport so moving. In my life in dance, I embody and witness so much far-flung material that sometimes I get lost trying to make sense of it. But volleyball's clear objective lets me admire its straightforward virtuosity and stylish biomechanics—truly the most beautiful of all the ball sports. What a dance.

To write this book, I imagined two beautiful girls with a secure relationship to their womanhood and unwavering commitment to the ball. Between drafts one season, I had a number of performances where I found myself absolutely not in the mood for the sold-out audience waiting on the other side of the curtain. I was warmed up but feeling cold. Then I thought of Six and Green and how they would understand my glamorous predicament. I set my unrelated feelings aside and put on a show. Thanking figments of my own imagination is sooo embarrassing and self-referential, but we had to start there.

Otherwise, so many real humans helped bring Six and Green to light in our world.

MY DEEPEST AND SPORTIEST THANKS TO:

- my ingenious agent, Danielle Bukowski, and the team at Sterling Lord Literistic, my brilliant editor, Alicia Kroell, and Cody Caetano at CookeMcDermid
- at Catapult especially, associate production editor tracy danes, copy editor Sarah Lyn Rogers, proofreader Mikayla Butchart, art director Nicole Caputo and cover designer Sarah Brody, publicist Megan Fishmann, and marketers Rachel Fershleiser and Ashley Kiedrowski

Plus, the full Catapult team:

Co-founder and CEO: Elizabeth Koch

Publisher/COO: Alyson Forbes

Editorial: Dan Smetanka, Kendall Storey, Alicia Kroell, Elizabeth Pankova

Marketing and Events: Rachel Fershleiser, Ashley Kiedrowski, Lily Philpott, Alyssa Lo

Publicity: Megan Fishmann, Lena Moses-Schmitt, Andrea Córdova, Vanessa Genao

Sales and Operations: Alyson Forbes, Miriam Vance, Katie Mantele, Alyzza Bowie

Design: Nicole Caputo, Farjana Yasmin, Victoria Maxfield, Eric Wilder

Production: Wah-Ming Chang, Olenka Burgess, Laura Berry, tracy danes

Also!

- Patrick Cottrell, Jasmine Gibson, Chantal V. Johnson, Lisa Ko, Andrea Lawlor, Sarah Thankam Mathews, Jeanne Thornton, and Tony Tulathimutte for your endorsements
- Cirsty Burton for taking my photos
- Cat Fitzpatrick and Casey Plett at LittlePuss Press, and Ryan D. Matthews with Rally Reading Series for handing a mic to early Six and Green
- Asian American Writers' Workshop, Bronx Council on the Arts, Lambda Literary, PEN/Bellwether, Periplus Collective, Poets & Writers, and Tin House

Last and most dearly:

- my early readers for your perspicacity and pep pep xoxo!
- the besties and party pals, teachers and guides, hot strangers and gym mates, fellow artists and #freelance-flailing colleagues, and my mutual cheerleaders too many to name—thanks for keeping us going. Thanks for keeping me beautiful and strong ♡

© Cirsty Burton

BENEDICT NGUYỄN is a dancer and gym buff. Between pistol squats and muscle-ups, she works as a creative producer in live performance. She's written for *The Baffler, BOMB, Los Angeles Review of Books, Vanity Fair, The Brooklyn Rail, The Margins,* and other publications. In 2022, she published *nasty notes,* a redacted-email zine on freelance labor. *Hot Girls with Balls* is her first novel.